THE GIRLS OF CANBY HALL

TROUBLEMAKER

EMILY CHASE

SCHOLASTIC INC.
New York Toronto London Auckland Sydney

ISBN 0-590-40711-2

12 11 10 9 8 7 6 5 4 3 2 1   7 8 9/8 0 1 2/9

Printed in the U.S.A.   01

First Scholastic printing, June 1987

THE GIRLS
OF CANBY HALL

TROUBLEMAKER

THE GIRLS OF CANBY HALL

Roommates
Our Roommate Is Missing
You're No Friend of Mine
Keeping Secrets
Summer Blues
Best Friends Forever
Four Is a Crowd
The Big Crush
Boy Trouble
Make Me a Star
With Friends Like That
Who's the New Girl?
Here Come the Boys
What's a Girl To Do?
To Tell the Truth
Three of a Kind
Graduation Day
Making Friends
One Boy Too Many
Something Old, Something New
Friends Times Three
Party Time!
Troublemaker

CHAPTER ONE

I don't believe it!" howled Toby Houston, sitting up in bed and staring out the window of Room 407. "This is too much! Way too much!"

"What are you griping about, Toby?" Andrea Cord peered out from beneath her pale pink comforter, horrified to see that it was not even six A.M. yet. Predawn. She'd always known that Toby was an early bird, but this — actually seeing it firsthand — was ridiculous!

Jane Barrett, the third roommate, remained silent as a mummy beneath her ivory blankets and quilts.

"It's snowing again — and hard," Toby said dismally. "It's almost spring and it's snowing. I mean, I never dreamed any place could have so much snow! Is this really Greenleaf, Massachusetts, or has Canby Hall been secretly transported to Alaska?"

"Oh Toby, you're just not used to a northern climate," Andy said, burrowing back down into her pillow. "I imagine nobody ever saw such a thing as a snowflake back there in Rattlesnake Gulch, Texas, hmmm?"

Toby threw her pillow at Andrea. "That's not true. Don't make fun of my hometown," she said, pretending to be insulted. "Not when you come from a place as weird as Chicago. A place where they don't have sense enough to keep their railroad trains on the ground. No, they have to put them way up in the air and call them something silly like 'els.'"

"Hey, don't *you* make fun of my Windy City," Andy scolded right back. "At least nobody in my hometown puts a tea bag on the ceiling." Pointedly Andy looked upward at the tea bag that had been hanging above Toby's bed ever since September. Nobody but Toby knew the reason for the tea bag, but it was by far the weirdest of all room decorations in Baker House.

Toby didn't answer that charge. Instead she sat on the edge of her bed and tested the floor with bare feet. She shivered.

"Snow," Toby grumbled. "And freezing cold floors. Ugh, what a way to live!" Toby's feet began rooting around to search for the fuzzy yellow slippers her father had given her at Christmastime.

"Face it. That's New England." Andy stretched her arms, but she had no intention of leaving her bed just yet. The three roommates of 407 Baker were great friends, but neither of Toby's roommates wanted any part of such early-bird activity.

Toby, the fuzzy slippers on her feet at last, stood up and stared at herself in Jane's full-length mirror. Her reflection showed a tall, slender girl with wild, curly red hair. Usually she didn't much worry about how she looked. Today, however, she thought she looked downright pale and peculiar.

"It's unhealthy, that's what it is," Toby muttered to herself. "All this winter and not enough getting outdoors."

Suddenly Jane was awake. Her blonde head popped out from beneath the covers. "What's the matter with you, Toby? It's not like you to be so negative."

"I don't know," Toby said honestly. She continued to stare at her pale reflection in the mirror. "I feel strange. I don't know what it is. I'm not homesick, exactly, but I feel almost, well, *snow*sick."

"Sick of snow?" Jane said. "I know exactly what it is, then! You have a classic case of the *Winter Blahs.*"

Toby turned to Jane, looking worried. "What is that? Some kind of influenza they get up here in the North?"

"Not the flu, Toby," Jane said, sounding like the proper, patient Boston girl that she was. "The Winter Blahs is not really a disease at all. It's more like a state of mind. A feeling of depression because winter is so long."

"Oh," Toby said, and suddenly a wide grin made her face look much brighter. "You mean like plain old cabin fever?"

"Right," Jane and Andy said at the same time.

"Well, it sure is a powerful disease," Toby said, sighing. "Or nondisease, as the case may be. Because I feel *plumb* weary from all this cold weather and snow and ice!"

Jane surprised them all by sitting straight up, looking almost wide awake, unheard of at that hour for Jane.

"There's only one cure for the Winter Blahs, Toby," she said in an excited voice. "And we're going to cure you."

Andy's dark brown eyes began to twinkle also. "I know what you're up to, Jane," she said. "You're thinking of a party. Am I right?"

"Righteo," Jane said, nodding. "A Winter Blahs party just to break up crummy old March — a month with no holidays at all."

"Well, there's Saint Patrick's Day," Andy reminded her roommate. She was quickly waking up. "But that's not exactly a holiday."

Toby was staring at the other two. "You guys are actually thinking of giving a party — for *me*?" She sounded absolutely incredulous.

"Sure," Andy said grandly. "Why not? This is your first year away from Texas. And there must be plenty of others who are feeling the winter doldrums. We'll invite all of Baker House! We'll have music and food and — oh, it'll be great!"

"And what do you do at these winter parties?" Toby asked with a real curiosity. "I know back home we sometimes have quilting bees on a chilly night, but —"

"*Quilting* bees?" Andy looked amazed. "You mean you Texas types sit around and make quilts?"

"Some do," Toby said defensively. "Some, like me, might just sit there and darn some socks, or mend some bridles, or polish boots. Sewing was never one of my favorite things."

"Well, well, well," Andy teased. "Someday we'll have to visit that part of Texas and see one of them thar quiltin' bees." She shook her head with laughter, her black hair still tousled from sleeping. But she was definitely awake with her enthusiasm over the idea of a party.

The three inhabitants of Room 407 were as different in looks as they were in personality. Jane Barrett was the only one of the three who came from a nearby city, Boston. She looked like the preppie of the group with her perfect posture and long, curly blonde hair, which she often swept up into a pony tail.

Jane's family was enormously wealthy, and Jane had been brought up to be a cool, reserved society girl. Since sharing Room 407 with Andy and Toby, however, Jane had loosened up a great deal.

Toby, born October Houston, and the quiet one of the three, hailed from Texas. Since her mother died some years ago, she'd been living a solitary life with just her father on their cattle ranch. And that was the reason he had sent her away to boarding school, "to learn to get along with humans."

Andy Cord, who came from a large, cheerful family in Chicago, was the chatterbox of the three. Andy was also the ballerina of the group. Her goal was to be a famous dancer someday. She was chic and feminine and had a wonderful hipness that came from growing up in Chicago.

The room reflected their different personalities as well. The walls were done in Wedgwood blue, Jane's favorite color. Originally Jane had expected to inhabit 407 alone, but along had come the other two with their possessions. Andy's ultramodern bedspread and throw rug, in diagonal earth-tone stripes, clashed terribly with Jane's antique crossstitch quilt and her blue and gray Persian rug.

That was bad enough. But then Toby had arrived with a spartan green Army blanket in her duffel bag and no decorations, except for her tea bag hung from the ceiling. Luckily, on a shopping trip in Boston earlier that month, Toby had found a rainbow store that appealed to her. Andy had helped her to choose a bedspread, a rainbow mobile, and other rainbow decor, so that her third of the room now had a style all its own, too.

Jane stretched and swung a long, slim leg out from under the covers. "A Winter Blahs party. What an idea," she said. "I'll ask Meredith today if it would be all right to use the dorm lounge." Meredith Pembroke was the new housemother of Baker House, ever since Alison Cavanagh had married a TV newscaster and gone off to attend graduate school in Boston.

Jane mused, "I wonder if Merry would let us hire Ambulance for the music?"

"Gosh, I wonder what made you think of that?" Andy teased. "Couldn't be because you'd like to have a certain lead guitarist and singer at the party, could it?"

"Could be," Jane said, blushing slightly. She had been dating Cary Slade, a rock musician from Oakley Prep, ever since school began. Cary was the most improbable boyfriend in the world for quiet, conservative Jane, but their relationship was proving that opposites did attract.

"Oh, this will be a boy-girl party?" Toby said, beginning to understand now. "Let's see. You'll invite Matt, probably, Andy. And Jane will have Cary there. That leaves me. . . . What do I do about a boy?"

"You've got your choice of two of them, actually," Andy told her. "You could ask Randy Crowell because you two have been such close friends."

Now it was Toby's turn to blush. She would have liked to be much more than friends with Randy Crowell, who lived and worked on his family's nearby horse farm. But he was twenty years old to her fifteen. Randy admired Toby and called her a red-haired little Annie

Oakley, but still he considered her a kid.

"Or," Andy went on, "you could ask Neal. That would be your best bet. He seemed to like you a great deal, the last few times you were together."

"That's true, Toby. Neal is crazy about you," Jane put in graciously. Neal, formally known as Cornelius Worthington III, had been Jane's boyfriend ever since pre-kindergarten days back home in Boston. But since Jane had become interested in Cary, Neal had turned his attention toward Toby.

"I don't know about any of this," Toby said, sounding confused. "I like Neal a lot, but asking a boy to be my date? Isn't that sort of backwards?"

"No!" Jane said. "How else can you get boys to a girls' boarding school if you don't invite them?"

"I don't know if I can call up Neal for a date," Toby said, shaking her head stubbornly.

"Nonsense. It's perfectly acceptable etiquette these days," Jane said. "You can and you will."

"Oh, I can't wait!" Andy declared, stretching. "I love to dance! I just can't wait to get out there and dance again."

"Well, slow down there, ballerina," Jane told her. "First we have to get this okayed by the authorities. And then we'll set a date and start making some arrangements."

"We can do it!" Andy sang out. "Meredith

won't say no. Not for a beautiful cause like this, to cure Toby's blahs. She just *can't* say no!"

"I'm afraid I can't say anything *but* no," Meredith Pembroke told them later that morning. The three girls had hurried up to the penthouse apartment on the fifth floor right before breakfast, hoping to catch their new housemother in a good mood.

Meredith Pembroke had started out on the wrong foot as housemother. A tall, thin woman in her late twenties, she had been determined to rule with an iron hand, and had spent her first weeks giving out more demerits than Baker House had ever seen in a whole century.

But in time, the severe Ms. Pembroke had realized the error of her strict ways and had slipped into being just plain Merry, the cheerful housemother who'd granted an Amnesty Day for all the demerits.

Merry's dark hair was no longer pulled back in a knot at the back of her neck. Instead, she was sporting a new body perm that the fourth floor girls had given her. Merry now had soft waves that came to her shoulders. She'd stopped wearing severe, gloomy suits and now appeared in colorful sweaters and sharp slacks. All in all, she'd improved greatly.

Unfortunately, Meredith was not a morning person. Today she looked bleary and weary, having spent much of the previous evening consoling a very homesick freshman girl.

"Don't say no to our W.B. party, Meredith, please," begged Andy. "I'll make you a cup of coffee. You just relax and think about it. Listen to Jane and she'll tell you all over again how depressed poor Toby is, and how much she needs a party!"

"But I don't have the authority to okay a big party in the dorm like this," Meredith said. "There's only one person who can give you permission, and you can guess who that is."

"Don't say it," begged Andy.

"Oh, no," Jane said, groaning.

All three of the girls said at the same time, "P.A.?"

"Ms. Allardyce, yes. I regret to say, she's the person you'd have to see about this party. Sorry, girls."

Andy flung herself down on Meredith's very formal striped couch. "We didn't know there would be such a hassle, just trying to give a little party."

"Well, it's not a little party when you're inviting boys and having a band," Meredith explained. "A little party is when you make popcorn or buy cupcakes or something for a few girls in your dorm room."

"We can give that sort of party any old time," Jane said. "We wanted to make this one sort of special, but we certainly don't want to face P.A. with our plans! She'd never agree."

Most of the students at Canby Hall were mildly terrified of the austere headmistress, Patrice Allardyce, whom they called "P.A." secretly. They all managed to avoid her as much as possible.

Toby sighed deeply. "We'll never have our party now," she said sadly. "And I was looking forward to it so much."

"Oh, Toby," Andy murmured in sympathy.

"That does it," Jane said fiercely. "Don't you worry, Toby, we *will* have the W.B. party! One way or another, we'll manage to talk to Ms. Allardyce."

"Brave words," Andy said. "Bravely spoken!"

CHAPTER TWO

"A Winter Blahs party? What a super-fantastic idea," exclaimed Maggie Morrison a short time later. Maggie, the next-door neighbor of the 407 roommates, was in the dining hall line with Andy, Toby, and Jane.

Maggie looked adorable this morning in denim engineer pants and a bright red sweater. Her huge glasses were perched on a freckled nose, and her dark hair made a fuzzy halo around her head.

"Yes, we thought the party would be fun," Andy said. "Our only big problem is that we have to approach P.A. about it. Hey, is this breakfast or some kind of *torture* lineup?"

Andy stared at the steam tables full of something mud-brown and gloppy. She couldn't believe that any sort of food could look so absolutely terrible. "What is that, anyway?" she politely asked Joanne, who was serving from behind the table.

"Oatmeal," Joanne said with a shrug.

"Oatmeal?" All the girls on the line gasped.

"Yeah." Joanne leaned forward a little bit and whispered, "I really think they burned it in the kitchen, so they poured in some molasses and other stuff and are calling it Oatmeal à la Canby."

"Appropriate," Jane said dryly, as she moved on toward the plain old toast. "Oatmeal à la Canby. Brown, burned, and utterly unappetizing. Most appropriate."

"So tell us more about this party you're planning." Dee Adams, Maggie's roommate, was finished working at the doughnut machine and hurried over to join her friends for breakfast. "Is it just for Baker House?"

"Yes, we think so," Jane answered. The five friends were heading now toward a favorite table near the south wall of the dining room. The dining hall was an airy, cheerful place with one whole wall of glass. Today the snow falling outside contrasted cheerily with the dozens of green, leafy plants arranged inside the windows.

"Toby has this major case of the Winter Blahs," Andy told Dee. "She actually wondered this morning if Canby Hall was in *Alaska*. So we thought the party ought to be in her honor."

Toby smiled proudly at that, and Dee pretended to pout.

"Well, how about me?" Dee asked. "Don't I deserve a party, too? This is my first eastern winter, too, you know." Tall, sunny-blonde Dee hailed from Laguna Beach, California, and was the very picture of a typical California girl.

"Sure," Jane said, smiling. "We'll have the W.B. party in honor of you, too, Surfer Girl."

As the five friends talked excitedly about their party plans, they never noticed that only one table away, Gigi Norton and her only friend, a quiet girl named Yolanda York, sat listening.

"Do you hear what they're talking about?" Gigi demanded of Yolanda. Gigi Norton was a black-haired, somewhat athletic girl who lived in Addison House. She was fond of sophisticated makeup to go with her sophisticated self-image. Jane had once roomed with her and still thought of her as Gigi (The Worst Person in the World) Norton, a true troublemaker.

Yolanda was methodically working her way through a bowl of the brown oatmeal. Yolanda was probably, Gigi thought in annoyance, the only girl in all of Canby Hall who had chosen the atrocious mixture for breakfast. But then Yolanda was not very discriminating.

"What?" Yolanda said.

"Wake up, Yo, will you?" Gigi snapped. "Someone's planning a party, and I don't think I'm included."

"But Gigi — " Yolanda wanted to tell Gigi that neither of them was friendly with the girls at the next table.

"Hush, I can't hear!" Gigi did not like the fact that Jane and her friends were among the most popular sophomores at Canby Hall. She didn't like Jane any more than Jane liked her.

"Giving a party, are they?" Gigi murmured. "Well, I'll show them they're not the only ones who can plan a party."

Yolanda's eyebrows went up as she began to comprehend at last. "We're going to give a party?"

"*I* am," Gigi corrected coldly. "And it's going to be the biggest party anyone ever gave at this moldy old school."

"Oh, wonderful, Gigi." Yolanda stared in admiration. "But, who are you going to ask to your party?"

"I'll decide that later. Maybe the whole school, we'll see. But first I'll have to wire to my parents for more money." Gigi stopped.

"Do you know where your parents are?" Yolanda asked.

"Of course I do!" Gigi looked furious at the question. "Well, at least, sort of. Last I knew they were headed for a jungle in Kenya or somewhere. But I'm sure they left some way to get in touch with them."

"Oh. Maybe with their agent?" Yolanda guessed. She knew that Gigi's parents were busy, well-known photographers, a team. Their profession took them to all sorts of places around the globe. Yo knew also that Gigi didn't have an awful lot of contact with her parents.

Voices from the next table drifted toward Gigi and Yo.

"Oh, Toby, you're going to feel one hundred percent better after this party!" Gigi knew that was Jane Barrett's voice, and instinctively she tightened her lips in a grimace. She was unable to stand it any longer. She stood up and sauntered over to the next table. Yo followed her.

"*Do* excuse me, but I couldn't help but overhear. You *were* loud — anyway, I thought you should know that *I*'m planning to give a party also," Gigi said smoothly.

"Oh, really?" Jane Barrett was the first to speak, and she sounded guarded. Polite, but wary.

"That's right," Gigi went on. "A huge party, catered, of course. I do hope it won't conflict with your little affair. I'd hate to *ruin* your party."

There was complete silence. Most of the girls were aware of what a problem Gigi could be. Her nasty remarks had cut into almost everyone's life at one time or another.

Still, Toby Houston thought it would be only common courtesy to say something.

"Sounds like you're sure making some fancy plans," Toby remarked in the politest voice she could muster.

"Yes, I am." Gigi's eyes swept around the table, studying the five friends. "You're invited, and I know you'll all want to be there because it's going to be the biggest thing of the Canby Hall social season."

"How interesting," Andy said. Social season?

"Yes," Gigi went on. "I'll be hiring a hall and of course serve the best food. My parents told me to go ahead and do whatever sort of entertaining I wanted here at this hick school."

"Now just a minute there, Gigi," Jane protested. "There's no reason to start insulting Canby Hall. Some of us happen to love it here, you know."

Gigi gave Jane a withering look. "I suppose some of you do. I suppose you don't know any better." She sighed theatrically. "Ah well. At any rate, I expect my party will be held this coming Saturday, if I can get all the arrangements made in time."

Gigi waited for comments, but none was forthcoming. "Well?" she finally said. "That's not the date of your little Baker House party, is it?"

"No," Jane said truthfully. "We haven't really set a definite date yet, but ours may be the following weekend."

The truth was, Jane and her friends were trying to think of a quick way to get out of this mess. They wanted nothing to do with Gigi Norton or any of her plans, but all of them were too polite to come right out and say such a thing. They were frantically searching their minds for excuses.

"Saturday night," Jane repeated, looking thoughtful. "Gosh, I have this feeling I have a date with Cary that night. Yes, I seem to recall that I do!"

Andy spoke up next. "That's right. I remember making a movie date with Matt, too, now that you mention it, Jane."

"No problem," Gigi said grandly. "You may bring your boyfriends to my party. They'll love it."

"Oh, I don't know. . . ." Jane looked stricken. "Cary's such a rebel, and doesn't really like catered parties."

"And Matt's pretty shy," Andy said.

Gigi's eyes suddenly flashed fire. "I'm sure your shy, rebellious boyfriends will *love* this particular party! It will be like no other." She paused for a moment of dramatic effect. "I've even chosen a costume theme for it, and it's one that will make everyone die laughing."

"What do you mean by that, a theme?" Toby asked.

"Just what I said. A theme," Gigi snapped. "Are you ready for this, girls?"

"We can't wait," Andy muttered, stabbing her fork at a piece of whole wheat toast.

"My theme is —" Gigi's eyes swept around the entire table, flickered briefly on the curious Yolanda, and then went straight to Jane Barrett.

"Yes?" Yolanda asked breathlessly.

"I am having a *Come as Someone You Hate* Party!" She paused.

No one said anything.

"Well?" Gigi demanded. "Can't you just see it? Everyone dressed up in costume and others trying to guess who they represent? It's funky *and* funny!"

"Brilliant, Gigi," Yolanda said in a whisper.

"Someone you hate?" Toby repeated, looking worried. "You mean, someone you really hate?"

"Of course," Gigi said impatiently. "You do know what the word *hate* means, don't you? Even in Texas?"

Toby refused to be baited.

"I don't know about this *hate* business," she said.

Gigi shook her head. "Look, it's quite simple. Everyone hates *someone*! So you merely dress up as that person and make a grand entrance at the party."

"No." Toby shook her head stubbornly. "I don't think I hate anyone."

"Oh, really." Gigi's laughter managed to reduce Toby's statement to something that a first-grader might have made. "Think of it this way. You could always wear a beige silk suit and pull your hair into a chignon."

"Why?" Toby said.

"You could come as P.A.," Gigi explained. "You do remember her — Patrice Allardyce, the headmistress of this dismal little school?"

"Why would I want to do that?" Toby persisted.

"Oh, give me a break. Absolutely everyone

hates P.A. So you come dressed as her and you'll get lots of laughs. That's what it's all about, getting laughs. Personally, I think it's going to be hysterical."

Toby stood up and fearlessly stared straight into Gigi's eyes. Every girl watching was full of admiration for her.

"Personally," Toby said with great care, "I think that's the most evil thing I ever heard of, Gigi."

"*What?*" Gigi's face turned red.

"That's right. Evil and downright tacky," Toby went on in a quiet, firm voice. "Where I come from, maybe we're not fancy or rich or sophisticated, but we sure do know about a thing called manners. And your party sounds like it has absolutely no good manners, Gigi."

"Why you — you ignorant little nobody!" Gigi stepped back in disgust. "No one could possibly take you seriously! A ranch sort of person who knows nothing except how to saddle up some silly bronco!"

"That's not true, Gigi," Jane said, also standing up. She stood beside Toby as a gesture of support. "We happen to have a lot of respect for Toby. We think that Toby knows a great deal about decency and common sense."

"Oh, pu-lease!" Gigi practically snorted.

Andy, Dee, and Maggie also pushed back their chairs and stood up.

"Toby's right, absolutely right," Andy said. "Evil is exactly the word for your party theme," Maggie put in. "Hating someone enough to dress up as that person — why, it's uncivilized."

"I'm surprised at you, Gigi," Dee said in a smooth voice, as though she'd always believed that Gigi was any ordinary good person. "You'll just have to come up with some other theme."

"I will not," Gigi said stubbornly.

"Well, we're sorry to say we won't be attending." Jane spoke firmly and coldly, as only she could do when she wanted to put a person in her place.

"That's right," came a chorus of voices from the rest.

Gigi shrugged. "You'll all be sorry," she said. "You'll be missing the greatest party this school ever saw. But that's *your* problem." She turned and walked away, with Yolanda trailing after her.

"C'est la vie," quipped Dee, who happened to be a terrible French student but who was able to muster up a few choice expressions when the occasion called for them.

"Yes, that's the way the cookie crumbles," said Andy with a shrug and a smile.

They were all off the hook. They didn't have to attend Gigi's party, after all.

"You will regret this, Toby," Gigi said as a parting threat. "You will all regret this."

And she turned and swept out of the dining hall.

"Gosh, I'm terrified," Andy said, raising her eyebrows in a comical gesture.

"She's a nasty person," Toby said, frowning. "I can't believe anyone can be so full of hate."

Jane shook her head and stared after the disappearing figures of Gigi and Yolanda.

"I'm afraid you haven't seen anything yet," Jane said, sounding a bit apprehensive. "When the Worst Person in the World is offended, she always gets revenge. Big time."

CHAPTER
THREE

"Oh, wait until you hear," Andy wailed later that day as she raced up to her roommates outside Baker House. "This is the worst news I've ever had to tell you."

"Well, what is?" asked Jane. "What can be so terrible?"

Andy kicked at a big mound of snow near the steps to the dorm. The snowfall had stopped by now, but the campus of Canby Hall was well covered with a fine, clean blanket of white.

"It's me. Someone did me in," Andy said woefully, "and I'm the culprit!"

"Whoa, slow down there, pardner," Toby suggested. "Tell us what's bothering you so maybe we can help."

"Oh, nobody can help," Andy said. She shifted a big load of books from one arm to the other. "I was such a dummy, spending so much time at the dance studio!"

"There's nothing stupid about that," Jane said. "You want to be a dancer, so that's what you do — spend time practicing at the dance studio."

Andy shook her head vigorously. "No, no, you don't understand. I completely forgot about my history assignment. I put it on the back burner of my mind and now, I just realized, it's going to be due next week!"

"Well, that doesn't sound so terrible." Toby bent down and packed a snowball, her hands encased in bright red mittens. "A history assignment shouldn't take too long."

"But this one will!" Andy groaned. " I have to write a long, fully detailed term paper on a subject in American history. We're talking many, many pages here."

"Oh," said Jane, understanding immediately. "And that means also that plenty of research is needed. The kind where you have to bury your nose in library books for days on end."

"Exactly!" Andy seemed to have bright tears in her eyes. "Mr. Lanahan told us about it long ago, and I should have been working on it all month, like the other girls in my history class. But I didn't, and now it's going to be due and I'm dead. Simply dead."

To illustrate her point, Andy fell back dramatically into the snow, landing in a snowbank that sprayed white flakes all over her plaid tights.

"But Andy," Toby said, trying not to laugh

at the sight. "I'm sure you can start working on it right away and get it done. What's your topic, anyway?"

"I chose black history in America," Andy said. "Because that interested me the most. In fact, one time Faith Thompson advised me to really get into the subject. But do you realize what a lot of research I'll have to do?"

"Sounds like quite a lot," Jane admitted. "But you're smart and full of energy. You can do it, Andy."

"Sure." Andy looked up at Toby with sad eyes. "But I won't have any time at all to spend on the party preparations. I mean, I'll be completely tied up for the next week."

"Oh." Toby suddenly looked sad, too. She had been counting on this Winter Blahs party an awful lot. In fact, it had been uppermost in her mind this entire day as she trudged from class to class.

I have no more reason to feel cabin fever, she had been telling herself even as she pulled her coat closer around her throat against the cold. *My two best friends are giving me a party!*

"Toby understands," Jane said soothingly. "And don't worry about a thing, either of you. *I'll* be able to go ahead and make plans for the W.B. party."

"You will, really, Jane?" asked Andy, looking relieved.

"Absolutely. It's in my Barrett blood after all." Jane smiled. "So do not worry about a thing, dear friends. I will produce a party that would do credit to any Barrett, living or otherwise."

"Whew, that's a relief," Toby said, once again breaking out into a grin. "I was afraid that the whole thing would have to be canceled, and I sure am getting hooked on the whole idea."

"Well, the party won't be canceled unless —" Jane stopped.

"Unless P.A. doesn't allow us to have it," guessed Andy.

"Uh-oh. And none of us has had the courage yet to go and ask her," Toby put in.

"Well," Jane said briskly to Andy. "Are you planning to sit there looking like a Snow Queen all afternoon, or are you going to come inside and get ready for dinner?"

"That depends," Andy said without missing a beat. "On what's for dinner, of course."

"No problem. I hear they've done something wonderful with pasta, for a change," Toby told her.

Andy made a face. "Oh, really? That sounds positively scary. *What* have they done with pasta?"

Toby grinned. "They've mixed fettucini with this morning's burned Oatmeal à la Canby — so now it's Oatacini à la Canby!"

"*Oh!*" Jane said, shuddering. "À la *ugh!*"

Toby had been teasing. The dining hall didn't have Oatacini à la Canby at all. The steam tables in the dining hall featured something called "Mrs. Merriweather's Medley," and it wasn't the usual gray color at all.

"It's *purple!*" Andy burst out as soon as she saw the dinner. "How do they get something edible to be purple in color?"

"Maybe they mixed plums with the meat sauce?" suggested Toby, half seriously.

"Calm down you two," Jane said sensibly. "There's always the salad bar, you know. We don't have to eat anything that looks like hot, congealed grape jelly." She set a glass of milk on her tray and moved along down the line quickly, as if afraid the purple stuff would send out tentacles to engulf her.

At the salad bar, Jane encountered Laura Lee Evans. Laura Lee was an unusually quiet girl from Baker House, and Jane really hadn't seen much of her this term. She thought it was rather odd, since Laura Lee lived right on the fourth floor down at the end room.

"Hi, Laura Lee," Jane said warmly. She noticed again how slender Laura Lee was, with pale skin that looked almost like porcelain, because it was so white and fragile-looking. In contrast to the pale skin, Laura had very black hair that swept gracefully to her shoulders. She wore, Jane noticed now, even more conservative clothes than Jane herself did: a quiet gray sweater, plain gray skirt, a demure white blouse. Laura Lee wore no jewelry except for a heart-shaped locket.

Strange clothes, Jane thought. Strange, for someone our age.

"Laura Lee, I wonder if you've heard yet about the Baker House party we're planning?" Jane asked on an impulse.

Laura Lee looked at her with big, dark eyes, almost like a frightened doe. "No," she said softly. "But I usually don't hear much of the talk that goes on around school."

"Oh, that's too bad. You're always welcome to walk down to our room sometime and sit and gab with us," Jane said. "We're always talking about things. Well anyway, I wanted to tell you that we're planning this Baker House party, probably for next weekend if we get permission, and — "

Laura Lee interrupted her. "I'm sorry, Jane, but I'm not really much of a partygoer."

Jane stared at Laura. "That's right, I haven't seen you at any of the parties we've had in the dorm. But Laura Lee, maybe you'd have fun at this one?"

Laura Lee picked up her tray and smiled sadly. "It's nice of you to bother, Jane," she said, "but I don't really think about things like parties." With that, she walked away to sit all alone at a table near the exit.

Well! Jane thought, feeling totally rejected. *You try to be nice to someone who seems lonely, and that's what you get!*

"You look madder than a cheated coyote," Toby told Jane as they met at the salad bar and began to load their plates with crisp, raw vegetables and lots of cottage cheese.

"Oh, no, not mad. Just puzzled," Jane said. "I'll tell you about it when we sit down."

And she did.

"I just don't understand why she's such a loner," Jane concluded, after she'd related the conversation with Laura to Toby, Andy, and Maggie. "I was thinking about it, and it occurred to me that I've never seen that girl with *anyone*. She's always by herself."

"How terrible," Andy said quickly. She was such a talkative, cheerful girl herself that she couldn't imagine anyone not having at least a few friends at school.

"Does she have a roommate?" Toby asked.

"No, I believe she has the only single room in all Baker House," Jane said. "And that's another mystery. I seem to remember Ms. Allardyce telling me that there were to be no singles for anyone this year."

"She sure did," Toby said, laughing. "And you were furious at first, weren't you?"

Jane had the grace to turn red. "Yes, and I was totally wrong, I admit it. Sharing a room with you two goons is much much better than being alone."

"Really? Even better than being alone with your beautiful Wedgwood blue decorating scheme?" Andy teased.

"And your perfect antique furniture?" Toby put in.

Jane put her hands over her ears and laughed. "Stop it, stop it," she begged. "Keep that up and you'll make me change my mind!"

"Anyway, about Laura Lee Evans," Maggie prompted.

"Yes, what about her?" Andy looked genuinely worried. "How can we find out what's making her such a hermit? And more to the point, how can we try to get her to open up a little bit?"

"You can't force someone until they're ready," Toby said wisely. "It's almost like that old saying about how you can lead a horse to water, but you can't make him drink."

Jane stared across the room. She saw Laura Lee sitting there, her hair shining almost blue-black in the dining hall light. Laura's back was straight and stiff, as if she was a very tense person. She was sitting totally alone with her dinner.

"We'll each have to work on this problem," Jane said decisively. "Do you all agree? We have to find out what's making that girl so unhappy."

"Yes," Toby said. "And I hope we do it before our Winter Blahs party. I'd like to have her there."

"Me, too," Andy said. "But I don't know if I'm going to be able to work on *anyone* or *anything*, except that term paper."

"Oh, poor Andy," Maggie said with real sympathy.

"I'm going over to the library right after

dinner," Andy said. "And I'll be there until it closes. I imagine that'll be a quieter place to work. Much quieter than Room 407."

"Gee, I don't know why you'd think that," Jane said innocently. "This was the night I was going to play my tape of the *1812 Overture*. What could be quieter than that?"

CHAPTER FOUR

Early the next morning Jane admitted to herself that she was worried about whether they'd be able to have the Winter Blahs party at all. Somehow, Jane was afraid it was not likely. She couldn't remember any Canby Hall students ever giving a boy-girl party in a dorm before, at least not one like she was planning. Most coed functions were school-run affairs, with plenty of chaperones and all the plans made by the school staff.

Oh, well. It was something she had to try, anyway. Jane knew that Toby was counting heavily on this W.B. party — maybe too heavily, actually. Toby was going to be terribly disappointed if none of it ever became possible.

The trouble was, when would be the best time to approach the headmistress to ask permission about the party? P.A. was cold and forbidding in the mornings. She was just as frosty in the afternoons.

And in the evenings? Forget it. Their headmistress usually looked quietly exhausted from a long day of dealing with students, teachers, and various Canby Hall matters.

Jane sighed. Perhaps, unlike Meredith, Ms. Allardyce was really a morning person at heart. In that case, why not try to catch her as she emerged from her house bright and early? It might just be a time when the headmistress felt fresh and ready to tackle a new day, and *maybe* there was a chance she'd say yes to Jane's request.

Jane was up and dressed early and had slipped out of Room 407 even before Toby woke up. She knew that Ms. Allardyce was an early riser who often breakfasted alone in her home before walking over to her office, before seven o'clock, to get an early start on the day's routine.

Jane planned to be waiting outside the headmistress' door when she emerged. It was a great plan, except for one thing: Jane hadn't counted on the unusual weather conditions.

"Oh, my gosh," Jane yelped the instant she walked out of the door of Baker House. "Ice! Pure ice!"

Jane skidded on the slippery walk, managing to keep herself from falling only by grabbing hold of the rail.

And then when she was stable, she stared. The whole campus appeared to be covered with a slick, almost invisible sheet of ice. Apparently rain had fallen during the night and had frozen on the ground. Sidewalks, stair rails, and tree branches sparkled in the early morning light. Jane could hear crackling and creaking sounds everywhere, as ice pieces broke from the strain of their own weight.

"This is terribly dangerous," she said aloud, even though no one was around to hear her. "Everyone will fall! Mr. Kreevitch should have been out already with the salt and sand spreader."

The handyman was nowhere to be seen, however. Jane looked desperately around at the treacherous conditions of the Canby Hall campus. This was a horrible situation. No one would be able to walk on the ice without getting hurt — and the worst part was that a person didn't see the ice at first glance!

Jane backed carefully into the dorm.

"Hey, what's wrong, Jane?" Toby was suddenly beside her, dressed warmly and looking ready for an early morning walk around the campus.

"You can't go out there!" Jane exclaimed, grabbing Toby by the sleeve of her jacket. "It's awful."

"What is?" Toby peered through the glass of the front door. "More snow? Doesn't matter. I can't get a worse case of the Winter Blahs, can I?"

"It's worse than snow," Jane said. "We've had an ice storm. It's pure ice, spread thin everywhere. The kind of weather that bad accidents are made of!"

Toby stared. "It really is. This is something I've never seen before. Look at those tree limbs bending over. Looks like the ice is going to kill some of those evergreens, doesn't it?"

"I doubt that," Jane said, "but it might kill some Canby Hall person. I think we ought to call Mr. Kreevitch, don't you?"

"If you say so," Toby agreed. The two girls went to the bank of phones on the first floor and checked in the campus phone book. Jane dialed the number listed for Canby Hall's resident handyman.

His wife answered. "Oh, Bernard is down sick today with a virus," she told Jane. "We've been trying to call Ms. Allardyce to tell her that Bernard can't possibly get to work today. But her telephone line isn't working. It must have been affected by the storm."

"But this is an emergency," Jane said. "We'd be glad to help, if we knew how. What shall we do about all the ice?"

"Let me check with Bernard," Ms. Kreevitch said, and turned away from the phone to ask some questions. She returned minutes later. "Bernard says there's a barrel of sand and salt at every dorm. Sounds to me as though you young ladies will have to spread it yourselves this morning."

"Well, that's fine," Jane said, "but what about the other buildings? Ms. Allardyce's house, for example?"

Ms. Kreevitch disappeared again. "Bernard says there is no barrel of sand at the head-mistress' house. And now he's worried about her."

"Well, tell Mr. Kreevitch not to worry," Jane said. "Not when he's so ill. Tell him we'll get some sand and go over to rescue Ms. Allardyce."

There was more consultation. "Actually, Bernard says that's not allowed because of insurance restrictions. But it does seem this is an emergency." Ms. Kreevitch hesitated. "Bernard says that's real nice of you, Miss — Ms. — "

"Barrett," Jane said, thinking about how odd it was that a Barrett of Boston would have to go out and sand the ice. Usually the Barretts had teams of servants to do things like this for them. "Tell Mr. Kreevitch to get well," she finished and hung up the phone.

Then she and Toby went to work. They found the sand barrels and began carefully spreading the mixture on all the sidewalks around Baker House. It was tedious work, and very unnerving, because each step they took could have sent them flying.

Slowly they worked their way along the paths that led to Ms. Allardyce's.

"Here's another pailful of sand," Toby said when they had reached Ms. Allardyce's front lawn. Her yard, like everywhere else, glistened with a thin, shiny coating of ice.

At that moment the huge walnut front door

of the house opened, and there stood Patrice Allardyce, poised and ready to step out on the front stairs.

"*Don't move!*" Toby shouted in the loudest voice she could manage. She'd sounded like a bellowing calf at roundup time, she thought, but she had to make sure Ms. Allardyce heard her.

"What in the world?" Patrice Allardyce stared at her two students but didn't move her feet. Good thing, too, Toby thought. Their headmistress was wearing high heels and if she'd moved even two inches she'd have come crashing down and possibly been really hurt, not to mention ruining that gorgeous beige wool coat with the oversized collar.

"Ice storm, Ms. Allardyce," called out Jane, waving her arms from the far edge of the lawn. "We're here with the sand and salt, so please don't move — yet!"

As quickly as possible the girls inched forward to spread the sand. Ms. Allardyce stood in her doorway, tall and regal, watching in absolute silence. Her face was as frozen as the ice that covered her home.

"Uh-oh. Are we in some kind of trouble, Jane?" Toby whispered.

"I hope not," Jane said. "She doesn't look too happy, though, does she?"

"Why would she be angry at us?" Toby asked in a voice too low for Ms. Allardyce to hear.

"Maybe because the Canby Hall insurance

doesn't allow the students to do dangerous work like this," Jane whispered, and Toby groaned.

At last they had succeeded in covering the ice with sand and salt, right up to the headmistress' door.

"There," Toby said in as calm a voice as she could muster. "Your walk is safe now, ma'am. And we're sorry if we did something wrong."

"We know students aren't supposed to be out doing this sort of thing," Jane began worriedly. "I suppose it's against all the insurance regulations and everything."

"But you see," explained Toby, "Mr. Kreevitch is sick and can't make it to work today, so we thought — " She stopped.

"How do you know Mr. Kreevitch is ill?"

"We called him a while ago," Jane said. "His wife said they'd been trying to telephone you, but your phone wasn't working."

Ms. Allardyce frowned. "And so you two decided to come out and play handyman yourselves?"

"Yes, ma'am," Toby said. "We didn't know if you had a substitute handyman or not."

"I want you two to come inside." Ms. Allardyce turned and disappeared inside her house, leaving Toby and Jane to wonder what was coming next.

"I suppose we have to go in there," Jane said.

"Unless we run away right now, and never

stop running," Toby answered, meaning it as a joke but deep down thinking it sounded like a great idea.

The girls went inside. The housekeeper, Ms. Hatch, instructed them to remove their boots and jackets. At length, they found themselves in Ms. Allardyce's morning room, a soft yellow room with tall windows and lined, ivory draperies. Through the windows was a view of the Canby Hall campus and the surrounding hills that was absolutely breathtaking.

"Please sit down, girls," Ms. Allardyce said, pointing to a small table with four chairs around it.

"Yes, ma'am," Toby said, biting her lip.

"Please don't look so terrified, October." Ms. Allardyce motioned something to the housekeeper. "Ms. Hatch will be bringing you some hot tea and a plate of croissants. I think you must be quite cold after your maintenance duties this morning."

"Er, yes, ma'am," Toby managed to say. Her teeth were chattering, but not from the ice storm outside.

Ms. Allardyce brought herself up straight and tall in her chair. "I must say that I have never been more proud of two Canby Hall girls than I am right at this moment," she announced.

Jane almost fell off her chair. Toby clutched the table as if to steady herself.

"You girls did a remarkable thing," Ms. Allardyce said. "You saw a potentially dangerous situation, and you immediately took steps to remedy it. Very, very commendable."

Toby and Jane sat dumbfounded while the cups of tea were carried in.

"You may have saved me from a terrible fall," their headmistress went on. "I was in a hurry and wasn't even looking at where I was walking, I'm afraid. And who knows where I might have ended up — in a hospital, perhaps."

Ms. Allardyce poured milk from a small, elegant pitcher. "Yes, and you made the campus safe for all the girls in the dorms as well. I am proud of you indeed."

"Thank you," Jane said quietly.

"No, thank *you*, Jane Barrett." Ms. Allardyce stopped and smiled, a thin but pleased little smile, and Jane knew that she really was impressed by the morning's work.

"And Toby Houston," Ms. Allardyce went on, turning to Toby. "It seems especially commendable that you were out there helping Jane, since this is your very first winter away from Texas. I'm sure you've never encountered a storm like this before."

"Yes, ma'am," Toby said, blushing. "But we just did what had to be done."

Patrice Allardyce nodded briskly.

"Now to change the subject a bit," she said,

"I understand from Ms. Pembroke, your housemother, that you girls have something that you wish to ask me."

Now Jane really could have fallen over with surprise. She'd had no idea that Meredith had talked to Ms. Allardyce!

"Something about a party, I believe?" Ms. Allardyce prompted. "A party of the sort that usually is not allowed in the lounges of our dorms?"

Jane took a deep breath and began talking fast before she could lose her nerve. She explained everything, and especially told how much the Winter Blahs party would mean to girls who were away from sunnier climates for their first time.

"There is a first time for everything," Ms. Allardyce said, leaning back. "Permission for your party is hereby *granted*. You have proven that you are not only brave and resourceful students, but also responsible ones."

"You really mean it?" gulped Toby nervously. "With boys and a band and everything?"

"I certainly do mean it. Meredith Pembroke is capable of helping supervise and chaperone, I am confident of that. So I want you to go ahead and enjoy your — what is it? Winter Blues party?"

"Winter Blahs, ma'am," Toby corrected.

"Hmmm, yes. Well, it sounds entertaining. And I'm sure that you will maintain the standards of Canby Hall in making it an excellent antidote to the Winter Blahs." Ms. Allardyce smiled almost warmly and lifted her tea cup.

They had actually received permission for the party!

CHAPTER FIVE

"*They* had to get permission from Ms. Allardyce for their party."

Gigi and Yolanda were hiking around the Canby Hall pond, which was frozen solid. The campus looked especially pretty with the ice, but Gigi was not looking at the majestic evergreens or the frost sparkling on lilac bushes.

"They were pretty smart to get P.A.'s permission, weren't they?" Yolanda asked.

"No, they're being juvenile," Gigi snapped. "I don't have to ask permission for *my* party, because I rented that party room in Greenleaf."

"It's just a back room at Pizza Pete's," Yolanda said, looking puzzled.

"I know!" Gigi looked angry. "I know it's not the Auberge, or the Greenleaf Inn, but it's what my budget would allow."

"You never could reach your parents, huh?"

"No. But that doesn't matter." Anyone who

had seen Gigi's face at that moment would have known, however, that it did matter, very much. She was a girl who seldom heard from her parents, and even when she did, it was just a quick note with no return address. Lila and Len Norton were on the move at all times, it seemed. "Have Cameras, Will Travel" was their motto, one that left little time for their only child.

"Everyone likes pizza in this hick school," Gigi went on. "So Pizza Pete's is a logical place to give a party, and not in some dumb lounge in Baker House!" Gigi was still burning over the refusal of the 407 girls, and their two friends, to attend her party.

"What about the invitations, Gigi?" Yolanda asked.

Gigi pushed the branch of a spruce tree out of her way. "I was thinking I'd put up announcements, instead. One on the bulletin board of each dorm. That way all the students will read about the theme of my party and have a good laugh."

"It is funny, Gigi. Come as someone you hate." Yolanda was chuckling.

"Of course it is! Too bad Toby had to argue about it. She'll find out what happens to meddlers."

"What do you mean, Gigi?"

"You just wait and see," was the prompt reply.

Minutes later, Toby Houston and Dee

Adams appeared at the edge of the same pond, both looking apprehensive. They were dressed in more winter clothing than anyone had ever seen before — earmuffs, scarves, heavy mittens, and even triple pairs of socks.

Gigi hastily pulled Yolanda behind a large hemlock tree to watch and listen.

"Well, Toby?" Dee asked fearfully. "Do we really want to go through with this?"

"Yes," Toby said. "I'm determined. Aren't you?"

Dee put out a mittened hand to touch the ice on the pond. "I'm scared silly, that's what I am. I've never gone out on a frozen pond in my life. I mean, these things just don't exist in Laguna Beach, California."

"Well, same with Texas," Toby said. She held up a pair of shining white ice skates. "But Jane lent me these skates, and I really want to give them a try."

Dee was holding ice skates, too. "And I borrowed mine from Amy, but I sure wish we had some northerner here to show us what this sport is all about."

Toby sat down on a rock and began to take off her winter boots. "You know, I really *begged* Andy to give us a few minutes of her time," Toby said with some bitterness. "She could have spared a little time just to teach us how to skate."

"Andy's too busy, huh?" Dee sounded sympathetic. "I know how it can be. When you have a huge term paper due, you can't slack off for even one hour."

Toby sighed. "I know it's unfriendly of me to think this way, but Andy could stop with that term paper once in a while. I mean, she's being so obsessive about it!"

"That's how it is though, Toby, and Andy has to do it." Dee struggled with the laces on her skates. "Boy, this sure is nothing like roller skates," she murmured. "We Californians live on roller skates, but these are weird contraptions!"

"They're harder to put on than I thought," said Toby, grunting. "But I figure, what's the point of going to boarding school in Massachusetts if we don't try this business at least once?"

"Right. If only we had someone here with us," Dee said. "Well, Maggie couldn't help us because she had a makeup test in chemistry. So where was Jane today? Why couldn't she give us a few pointers?"

"Oh, Jane is at choir practice right now. And then she's running around making arrangements for the party. Everything's going to be top secret, except that she has to let Meredith in on her plans, of course." Toby grunted as she bent over the other skate. "Jane's a true friend," she added.

Dee stared at Toby. "And you're saying that Andy is not?"

"I'm not saying anything," Toby asserted. "Just that some people — some *certain* roommates — shouldn't have let all their history assignment go the way they did."

Dee looked shocked. "Then you did mean Andy."

"I guess so. I was counting on both Jane and Andy planning the party. I know it's silly, but this Winter Blahs party is awful important to me."

"Maybe *too* important, Toby."

"Well, it's special to have a party given in your honor." Toby grinned. "Don't forget, I even threw my own birthday party, back in October!"

"Yes you did, but that was only because no one knew the date of your birthday," Dee reminded her. "You know Andy hates being rushed with this term paper just as much as you hate her doing it. And she would be helping with the party if she could."

"And our skating lessons?" Toby added. "There. I've got the persnickety things on at least. Let's go, Dee."

Watching from behind the hemlock tree, Gigi and Yolanda weren't about to offer any advice. They were looking forward to The Big Tumble.

And they didn't have long to wait.

"Oh my gosh! This is impossible!" Toby shrieked as she flailed her arms in the air, feeling her ankles give way as the blades of the skates took a major slide forward.

"Toby, help!" Dee called out desperately.

"I can't! I'm down!" Toby informed her.

Dee was trying desperately to grab onto a tree branch that was jutting out over the ice. "I can't get it. Oh, Toby, this is harder than riding the surf! I have no control at all!"

"Tell me about it," Toby said glumly. She was sprawled ungracefully across the ice, wondering how in the world a person ever could get up from her position.

"No, you tell *me* something," Dee howled, doing a weird dance in her efforts to keep on her feet. "Toby — does it hurt to fall down?"

CRASH! Dee found out before Toby could answer.

They were both flat out on the ice. Facing each other, Toby and Dee did the only thing they could do — laugh, long and loud. Somehow it made things seem better.

"What is this? Elephants on ice?" Gigi said scornfully as she stepped out from behind the tree. "Why don't you just give up?" She and Yolanda turned and walked disdainfully away.

After they were gone, Toby and Dee, still sprawled out on the ice, began to giggle even harder than before.

"Is that Gigi's idea of getting revenge?" Toby managed to ask, in between gulping laughter.

"Oh, no," Dee said, suddenly sobering. "She can be worse. What I don't like is that she must have overheard our whole conversation."

"So?"

"So that's the kind of stuff she uses, Toby."

Toby thought about that for a minute. "Well, I don't see how Gigi can use something like that."

Dee stared off toward the snowy woods path where Gigi and Yolanda had just walked off.

"I hope I'm wrong about her," Dee said in a worried voice.

CHAPTER
SIX

"How was the ice skating?" Jane asked when Toby came limping back into Room 407 later that afternoon.

"Don't even ask," Toby groaned. She put the ice skates down on the rug next to Jane's bed. "Thanks so much for letting me borrow these skates, Jane, but it was a disaster. Dee and I must have given it about eighty-eight tries, but they all ended up with us flat on the ice."

"Well, you can't expect to become the Queen of the Ice in one afternoon." Andy looked up from her spot at her desk where she was surrounded by reference books, file cards, and stacks of scrap paper.

"We might have had more luck if a certain person could have gone with us," Toby muttered, plopping herself down on her bed, face up. "Someone from Chicago, that is, where everyone knows how to skate."

Andy looked surprised. "Are you mad at me, Toby? You know I couldn't go to the skating pond with you."

Toby stared up at the tea bag hanging from the ceiling. "I know you *said* you couldn't go. You were so extremely busy with your history report."

"Hey, Toby, what is this?" Jane demanded. "You can't possibly be angry with Andy! You know schoolwork is the first priority of all of us here at Canby Hall."

"I suppose so," Toby said reluctantly. "But sometimes friendship can be a priority, too."

"Be reasonable, Toby." Andy turned around to stare at her roommate. "I mean, I don't believe this! Here I am swamped with work, from Booker T. Washington to Sojourner Truth to Harriet Tubman, even to Joe Louis and Chubby Checker! You should be feeling sorry for me, not angry at me."

When Toby didn't answer, Jane spoke up quickly. "Toby *is* feeling sorry for you, Andy, I can tell. She's just a grump today because, on top of her Winter Blahs, she now feels like a failure on the skating pond."

"Is that right, Toby?" Andy asked.

"Yeah, something like that," Toby admitted. "But I really was wishing you had come skating with us, Andy. And you know what? Dee says this W.B. party is getting too important to me."

"She may be right," Jane said briskly. "But I'll tell you, the whole thing is going to be well worthwhile. I won't give any secrets away, of course, but. . . ." Jane's eyes sparkled with pleasure and anticipation.

"Hey, now that we have Ms. Allardyce's permission and all, we have to ask some boys, don't we?" said Andy. "I guess I'll give Matt a call, although I sure do wish I could import Steve, from Chicago." She had a dreamy expression on her face.

Andy had been fond of Matt, who was a student at Oakley Prep, for several months now. But then over Christmas break, when she'd gone home to work in her parents' restaurant, she had had a sudden romantic rush from Steve, a part-time waiter there.

"You and your multitude of boys," Jane said, chuckling. "I'm glad I only have Cary to invite. And Toby — you have to get busy and invite Neal to our party."

"I don't think I can do it, Jane," Toby said seriously. "I've never invited a boy before, and it sounds — well, really scary."

"That's silly," Jane said. "There's nothing to it."

"I think I'll go to the first-floor phones and call Matt right now," Andy said, suddenly leaving her desk to search for coins for the pay phones. She found them and left the room like a whirlwind.

"Sure," grumbled Toby. "She has time to run and call up a boy, but not one minute to show us how to skate. Or to help with the party."

"Toby," said Jane firmly, giving her the Barrett of Boston cold look. "You stop that whining this very minute. I've never heard you being such an old grouch! It's terrible. That's no way to run a friendship."

"I'll stop, I'll stop," Toby said, sitting up. She stared at the pile of papers on Andy's desk. "But that still doesn't mean I have to be happy about this history project of hers."

Toby became even more depressed a little later, when she had an unexpected phone call, on a downstairs phone, from Randy Crowell.

"Hi, Toby," Randy said, and Toby's heart jumped almost a mile. No matter how often she reminded herself that she and Randy were "just friends," his voice always had this devastating effect on her.

He went on, "I couldn't get through on the phone in your room, so I thought I'd give you a call on your pay phone to see how you're coming along in this cold weather. Haven't seen you in a few weeks. How are you making it, pal?"

"Good, I suppose," she said quickly. "Well, not exactly. My friends decided I have the Winter Blahs."

Randy laughed heartily. "That's too bad, kiddo. But the weather has been really rough these past few weeks. I guess you're dreaming about spring and some rides on Maxine."

Maxine was a horse that Toby had helped to tame for the Crowell horse farm. Toby had named the horse after her horse at home, Max.

"I sure am," Toby said. She realized that the hand clutching the phone receiver was perspiring. An idea had come to her and she was suddenly nervous. She wouldn't *have* to call a boy to ask him to the party. Randy had called her, hadn't he?

"Uh, Randy?" she began.

"Yes?"

"I was just wondering. Are you . . . are you doing anything a week from Saturday night? Because we're, that is, Jane is giving a special party for all the girls in Baker House and their guys." She hesitated. "That is, it's going to be called a Winter Blahs party, you see. . . ."

"Toby, are you trying to invite me to your party?"

"Yes," she said with relief. "I am. Randy, would you like to come as my guest?"

There was a long silence, and Toby's heart sank. "Toby," he finally said. "I wish I could say yes to you. But you know we've talked about this before."

"Oh Randy, listen," Toby argued. "You're my best friend here in Greenleaf, and the only friend who understands about horses and ranches and stuff."

"Toby." Randy's voice was quiet and firm. "I can't go to a party with you. I'm terribly sorry. It would be too much like a date, and you know we don't have a dating kind of relationship."

Toby sighed. She said, "And besides, you vowed never to get involved with another Canby Hall girl, didn't you?"

"Yes, because anyone at Canby Hall is too young for me. You have someone else you can ask, don't you, Toby? That Neal from Boston — he's more your own age, isn't he?"

"Oh, sure." Toby forced herself to make her voice light, even though she felt utterly dejected inside. "I just thought I'd try my luck with an eastern cowboy first."

Randy laughed, and the tension seemed to be dissolved. They talked for a while about Maxine and the other horses, and agreed they'd go for a long trail ride as soon as the cold weather broke.

Toby hung up feeling worse than ever. It was great that Randy had thought to give her a call, but it didn't solve her dilemma of a date for the W.B. party.

"Gosh, that's simply a shame," a sarcastic voice said from around the corner. Gigi Norton again! "Golly, I'm heartbroken for you. You got turned down by your handsome eastern cowboy, huh?"

Now Toby got really furious. "What are you doing here in our dorm?" she demanded. "You belong in Addison, don't you? Who gave you the right to come snooping around in Baker House?"

"Tut tut," said Gigi. "I'm here to post the invitations to my party. Nothing wrong with that."

"You're just here to snoop!" Toby accused again.

"Well, I do learn all sorts of interesting things that way," Gigi said. "Like how not to get a date."

With that she turned and left the dorm, leaving Toby shaking with rage.

"Don't worry about her," Maggie said a short time later when she was visiting in Room 407. "Gigi's a creep and I don't think anyone's going to her stupid party."

"No one?" asked Toby.

"No one who has any sense of decency," Maggie said. "I mean, that idea is just so disgusting, dressing as someone you hate! I heard at least ten or fifteen girls discussing it and saying they wouldn't be caught dead there."

"Well, she'll blame the whole thing on me," Toby said, sounding a little worried. "She's been after me in a big way, ever since I was the first one to tell her her idea was evil."

"Do not fret, people," Jane said. "Our party will more than make up for any problems Gigi can cause in the meantime."

"Can you all please keep down the noise?" Andy begged suddenly, still buried in books and papers at her desk in the corner. "I mean, I'm going crazy here!"

"Oh, sorry, Andy," Jane and Maggie said at the same time.

"It's not easy, you know," Andy called out, not even turning around. "Black history covers an awful long time. I think I bit off much more than I can chew!"

"You can do it, Andy," Jane encouraged her.

Toby said in a worried voice, "I only hope you don't miss the W.B. party."

Andy did turn around now. "Of course I won't miss the party, Toby. Are you crazy? I'd never miss it!"

"Toby Houston!" Suddenly and fiercely, Jane grabbed Toby by the shoulders and pushed her out of the room, with Maggie following along behind. Jane continued to push Toby all the way down the hall and into the fourth floor bathroom.

"Hey, why are you pushing me around?" Toby wailed as she felt herself being jammed up against the line of sinks.

"Why?" Jane sputtered. "Because I want to stop this trouble before it goes any farther."

"What trouble?" Maggie asked in all innocence.

Jane pointed a finger toward Toby's nose and wagged it like a traffic cop. "You are *not* to keep picking on Andy about her history paper, Toby, do you hear?"

"I hear," Toby said, sheepishly.

"I know," said Jane, "that you resent it a

little that Andy isn't able to help me with the party. But Andy can't help it, and anyway the party plans are going along JUST FINE."

"They are?" Toby asked.

"Oh, sure," Maggie said cheerfully. "I'm being Jane's assistant."

"I didn't know that."

"Sure. And we have everything under control."

"You do?" Toby began to look really happy.

"Yes!" said Jane.

Just then the bathroom door swung open. Laura Lee Evans walked in, carrying a spray can of mousse and a styling brush.

"Oh," she said, looking flustered. "I didn't know anybody was in here."

"No problem," Jane said quickly. "Come on in."

But Laura Lee backed up a little, looking paler than usual.

"I don't know."

"Hey, is that mousse?" asked Maggie, bouncing forward toward Laura Lee. "Why not let one of us help you? We love to style each other's hair!"

"No, no," Laura Lee said. "I don't, I really wasn't planning, I just happened to walk out of my room carrying these."

"Laura Lee, what is it?" Jane asked abruptly. "Why are you so afraid of people?"

Laura Lee turned big violet eyes toward Jane. "I'm not," she denied. "I just like to be alone."

"But that's crazy," Maggie said in her usual blunt way. "No one should be alone all the time. You came to Canby Hall to be with other girls, didn't you?"

"No," Laura Lee said suddenly. "I came to Canby Hall because I had to."

"You had to?" Now Toby was intrigued.

"Canby Hall is a tradition in my family," Laura Lee said. "My mother attended this school, and so did my grandmother and several of my aunts."

"Oh. A tradition," Toby said, nodding. "This place is full of traditions."

"And another one is that Canby Hall girls should try to make friends," Jane said, pressing relentlessly on.

"I can't," the girl said in a quivering voice. "I can't, so why don't you just leave me alone?" She turned and went out the bathroom door, fleeing down the hall toward her lonely room at the far end.

The other girls looked at each other.

"Well, that was a raging success," Maggie said.

"We really tried, didn't we?" Jane asked, sounding dismal and discouraged.

"I can't understand her," Toby muttered, throwing her hands up.

"Maybe she doesn't want us for friends," Maggie said with a devilish look in her eyes. "Maybe we look like a pack of aliens to her, you know, like from Mars or Saturn."

"Well, you could have hidden your

antennae, Maggie," Jane said, pointing to Maggie's curly hair. "And with those big glasses, you look like you're beaming in on some spaceship frequency."

"That's nothing," Maggie said. "It's just lucky she didn't see my webbed feet!"

CHAPTER
SEVEN

Well, I don't know what we can do about Laura Lee just yet," Jane said glumly. "But I think there's one thing we do have to do about you, Toby Houston!"

"What? You aren't going to push me all around again?" Toby asked. "I've promised to behave."

"We have to get you your date for the W.B. party, don't we?" Jane said. "You should have called Neal in the first place."

"I know, but I'm afraid to call a boy for a date," Toby admitted.

"But it must be done!" Maggie declared. "You're right, Jane, we have to drag her to the phones and see that she calls Neal!"

"Okay, but you don't have to drag me," Toby said in a gesture of mock surrender. "I'll go peacefully."

The three of them trooped downstairs to the phones on the first floor.

"Now I'll dial Neal's number," Jane said. "But you have to talk to him."

"You know his dorm number?" Maggie asked, impressed.

"Oh, sure," Jane said. After all, she and Neal had been friends absolutely forever. She clicked the push-buttons on the phone with efficient precision.

"Here you go," Jane said, handing the phone to Toby.

"I *can't*," Toby whispered, but she put the receiver to her ear anyway. She heard the ringing on the other end. And she felt the thump-thump-thump of her heart as it slammed against the ribs in her chest.

She was so nervous that she thought it was Neal's roommate who had answered the phone.

"Is Cornelius there?" she asked. "I mean, Nealonius? I mean — oh, never mind."

"This is Neal," said the smooth, puzzled-sounding voice on the other end. "And who is this? You sound like Toby to me. Am I right?"

"Y — yes," was all she could manage.

"Why, Toby, what a nice surprise," Neal said. "To tell you the truth, I was just thinking about calling you."

"You were?"

"Yes. I was wondering when we could see each other again."

"Really?" Toby was flabbergasted.

"Sure." Neal's voice sounded so friendly

and sincere that Toby forgot all about her nervousness.

She should have known she could call Neal. They'd had a terrific time a few weeks ago in Boston when Toby and Andy went to visit Jane's house in Boston. And then Neal had come to visit her recently when she'd been in the school infirmary with a badly sprained ankle.

"Neal, I have something to ask you," she blurted out in a tumble of words, before she could lose her courage.

"Ask away," he told her.

"Well, we're having this party next Saturday night in our dorm, and I wondered — "

"I'd love to come," Neal said, interrupting her.

"What? You would?"

"That *is* what you were going to ask, isn't it?" He sounded worried. "Or were you going to ask if you could borrow my stereo for the party, or my mother's cut-glass punch bowl, or something like that?"

"No, no." Toby laughed. She felt wildly happy all of a sudden. "Of course I was going to ask you to be my date."

Date, she had managed to say. And it wasn't that terribly difficult! She turned to look at Jane and Maggie, who were waiting anxiously, and she winked an eye.

"I'd love to be your date," Neal repeated. "What time is the party?"

She told him. And then she asked anxiously, "Do you want to speak to Jane, to find out anything else?"

"No," Neal said. "I found out everything from you, Toby. And you're the only one I need to talk to."

"Really?"

"Sure. You can say hi to Jane for me. Well, I'll see you then," Neal said.

"Yes," she answered, in a daze. "Bye."

When the receiver was down, all three girls let out a whoop of joy.

"You did it!"

"He's coming!"

"I did it," Toby said. "And he's coming!"

"Well, well, so she managed to get herself a date," Gigi Norton said.

"Yeah, I heard the whole thing," Yolanda York told her. The two girls were sitting in Gigi's room a little later. "I was sitting behind the pillar in Baker House when they came down the stairs."

"Good," Gigi said impatiently. "So, it's Neal Worthington she asked next. And he finally said yes."

"You know him?" Yolanda asked.

"Of course I do!" Gigi stared at one of her long fingernails. "Didn't I room with Jane Barrett last year? I even know Neal's address at that fancy school he goes to."

"What are you going to do with his address?" Yolanda asked.

Gigi reached out and took some stationery from a drawer in her desk. She slipped a piece of the paper into her portable electric typewriter, smiling the whole time she did so.

"Write him a letter, of course," she said. "A ve-ry, ve-ry interesting letter. And this ought to put a crimp in the pitiful party plans of October Houston!"

"So now we all have a date for our W.B. party, right?" Jane asked when they had gone up to Room 409, Maggie and Dee's room. It was a cheerfully sloppy room, full of Maggie's books and magazines and Dee's piles of brightly colored clothes. On Dee's side of the room, the walls were covered with surfing posters.

"The five of us have, anyway," Maggie said. Maggie had a date with a boy named Billy Dunstan, a sophomore at Oakley Prep. She'd met him at a mixer the month before.

Dee had invited a Greenleaf High School boy, Ed Morris, who also happened to have hailed from California originally. They had met one day outside the Greenleaf Travel Bureau, when both of them were staring through the window at a poster of San Simeon Castle in California. They had both admitted they were homesick for the sunshine of their home state, and that had been that. Instant friendship.

Andy of course had gotten a yes from Matt, who would be coming anyway because he did the lighting for Ambulance, the rock band. And Jane had had no trouble at all getting Cary Slade and his group, first, because Cary was crazy about Jane, and second, because even though Ambulance was good, they didn't get asked to play all that many gigs.

Dee was making some pencil marks on the wall above her bed.

"What are you trying to write there?" Toby asked.

"I'm not writing," Dee said, tossing her long mane of thick, blonde hair. "I'm considering painting a huge palm tree on this wall."

Maggie did a double take. "You're kidding, right?"

"No, I'm not. Why couldn't I paint a really sharp-looking palm tree right here?" Dee continued to sketch the leafy fronds of her fantasy tree across the beige wall.

"It would make you feel at home," Toby said, guessing. "And it would go with all those beach posters you have."

"Sure," Dee said. "And it would look great, with bright green enamel here on the palm leaves, and some brown enamel down here for the trunk."

"You're really artistic," Toby said in admiration. "But then, both your parents are artists, aren't they?"

"Yes."

"You're also pretty wild and crazy, Dee," Maggie said with a big grin. "But I think that must be the way to go here at Canby Hall. After all, if my sister Dana and her friends could live with black walls!"

"And their mattresses on the floor, like islands," put in Jane, with a shudder.

"Then why not a palm tree in 409?" Maggie finished. "Sure! Go for it, Dee!"

"Hmmm." Jane was staring at Dee and her palm tree for a minute. "You're giving me some ideas. . . ."

"What do you mean?" asked Toby.

"Never mind," Jane said mysteriously. "Just never you mind."

"I can hear the old wheels clicking in the Barrett brain," Maggie said, raising her eyebrows at Jane. "And I bet this is about the W.B. party, right?"

"You bet." Jane motioned Maggie to come out of the room with her. "High level strategy conference. Sorry, Toby," she said firmly. "You can't join us." And they disappeared.

"There sure are a lot of secrets around here these days," Dee said cheerfully. "What do you think, Toby? Do I draw a coconut right here, or not?"

Toby stared at the pencil sketch. "No, I think maybe a monkey. They belong in palm trees, don't they?"

Dee looked surprised. "Why yes, I suppose so, but why would I want a monkey?"

"So you can give it a face like Gigi Norton's," Toby said. "Is that terrible of me to say?"

"Well . . ." Dee said. "That girl *is* out to get you, Toby, and everybody around here knows it."

Toby sighed deeply. "I just wonder what she'll try to do."

"Don't worry about her. Whatever she does, we're your friends and we'll fix her wagon right back."

Toby's eyes misted with unexpected tears.

"Thanks, Dee," she said.

The next day Andy went into the Canby Hall library for about the twentieth time that week. The place was becoming a second home to her because of the history term paper. She found it quieter to work there on the round oak tables among the stacks of books.

Today she spotted a lone figure sitting at one of the library tables near the Biography section.

Laura Lee, she thought, remembering Jane's plan to try to befriend the strangely quiet sophomore girl.

"Hi there, Laura Lee," Andy called out briskly. She probably spoke a bit too loudly because the head librarian, Ms. Kenworthy, looked up and said, "Sssssh!"

"Oooops," Andy said, sitting down quite deliberately next to Laura Lee. "Guess I have to learn to keep my voice down in a library."

"Yes," Laura Lee muttered, not really looking at Andy.

"Say, we've never met formally," Andy said

with a smile. "I seem to know that your name is Laura Lee, but maybe you don't know that my name is Andy. Andrea Cord, from Chicago. I live in 407. And you and I are both in Mr. Lanahan's history course."

Laura Lee looked at her blankly. "Yes, I know."

"Whew, you're determined to make this hard for me, aren't you?" asked Andy. She started to spread out all her books and the millions of papers that contained notes for her history paper. "I'm not really here to pester you, you know. I'm working on my history paper. Is that what you're doing, too?"

"No, I finished mine last week," Laura Lee said.

"Lucky you! Well, what are you doing here then?"

Laura Lee hesitated for a minute. "I come here often. It's quiet. And it's nice. I like books a lot."

"Oh." Andy thought that was a little strange — not the part about liking books because she liked them herself, but coming to the school library on a regular basis for no real reason. Well, that just sounded to Andy like a way of avoiding people.

Andy wasn't about to give up on Laura Lee, however.

"I suppose I'm bothering you, sitting down here next to you like this," Andy persisted. "But that's how I am, friendly. My friends back in Chicago sometimes called me Andy the Moving Mouth because I'm always talking."

Laura Lee sighed and said nothing.

"Do you want to know my topic for the history paper?" Andy asked.

"Not really," Laura Lee said, but politely. She had her nose buried in a book of French verbs.

"It's black history," Andy said, undaunted. "A really hard topic, I'm finding out. I mean, I am *so* confused with all these people and all the important things they've done. Where do I begin? It's horrendous."

Laura Lee looked at Andy with a flicker of interest.

Then, unexpectedly, she ventured a comment. "Do you have anything in your notes about Mary McLeod Bethune?"

Andy's mouth fell open in amazement. Laura Lee had spoken!

"No! I forgot her," Andy said.

"Well, she's certainly a noteworthy black educator from South Carolina," Laura Lee said. "That's where I once lived, so that's why I've heard all about her. She not only started schools for black girls, she actually worked with President Franklin Roosevelt and received some big award."

"Here she is," Andy said, rapidly thumbing through one of her reference books. "I found her. I must have skipped right over her completely in my research. Hey, thanks, Laura Lee."

"You know," Laura Lee said, "you might have less trouble with your paper if you narrowed it down to a somewhat smaller topic. Like for instance, just write about black women in American history."

Andy's eyes widened with surprise. "That's a good idea. I appreciate it."

"You're welcome," the girl said. She began to gather her books, her purse, and her soft gray coat.

"Hey, you're not leaving are you?" Andy said in dismay. "We were just getting acquainted."

"You need some peace and quiet to do your paper," Laura Lee told her shyly. "And I have to do some things."

"What kind of things?" demanded Andy.

"Oh, clean my room. Wash out some stuff."

Just an excuse to take off, Andy thought, but there wasn't much she could do about it. Laura Lee was determined to leave.

"Thanks again for the help," Andy said as Laura Lee slipped out. But there was no answer.

CHAPTER EIGHT

So I suspect she's really a nice person." Back in 407 later that evening, Andy reported to her roommates the latest story about Laura Lee. "Imagine, she actually spoke to me, and gave me that great tip. Now I'm planning to change my report to black *women* in American history."

"That would narrow it down for you, wouldn't it?" Jane said, nodding with approval. "Might make it easier."

"It will make it a better paper," Andy said with a big sigh. "But nothing's going to make it easier. Anyway, I've already started some of the writing.

"Will your paper be done in time for the W.B. party?" Toby asked.

Andy bristled. "Are you still worried about that?"

"No, no, I'm not," Toby said quickly, seeing that Andy looked ready to fly off the handle.

"I was only concerned about you, Andy, and your tight deadline."

"Well, I know I'm going to make it, Tobe," Andy said. "And as for our W.B. party, I just know it's going to be terrific. But, dear roomies, I cannot sit and chatter, unfortunately. There's work to be done."

"I have biology to study, too," Toby said, opening her book to a diagram of a human skeleton. "Ugh," she said. "I don't know why I have to study all these crazy things."

"That's so you can learn the names of important bones," Jane told her with a devilish twinkle in her blue eyes.

"But why?" Toby asked, falling right into Jane's trap.

"Because some bones are vital. Like osteocranium." Jane winked toward Andy at this.

"Huh? There's no such thing," Toby said, looking down at her book. "At least, not in my diagram here. . . ."

Jane and Andy burst out laughing.

"*Osteo* means 'bone,' " Jane said.

"And *cranium* means 'head,' " put in Andy.

"So put 'em together, and you've got *bonehead*!" Jane said.

Toby blinked. "Well, what do you know?"

"You need to remember that one," Andy said, chuckling, "in case you're looking for a name to call Gigi sometime."

On Saturday morning, Jane walked to the Greenleaf Diner (sometimes known as the

GREAF Diner, because of missing sign letters). She was going for a cup of coffee and because Cary Slade worked there on weekends.

"Hi, Janie," Cary called out as soon as she entered the place. He looked different today, slightly neater than usual, Jane realized. For the first time, his longish blond hair was swept back neatly, and he wasn't wearing an earring.

"My goodness, Cary. Why are you looking so conventional?" Jane asked, doing a double take. Usually Cary was as offbeat as he possibly could be — a form of rebellion against his childhood upbringing in Boston high society.

"Oh, the boss wanted to see us all look more professional and sanitary," Cary said, his blue eyes twinkling. "Sometimes the Health Inspectors come in to check on things, and they don't like to see a counterman with long hair."

"And I'd say they're right, too," Jane said in her most exaggerated prim and proper voice. She sat down at a stool and began to rub her hands, which were freezing from the frigid temperature outside. "I'll have coffee please, Cary," she said.

"Sure," Cary said, pouring a cup for her. "And as for your remark — I don't appreciate it, Jane."

"What do you mean?" She looked at him in amazement.

"There's one thing I hate even more than easy-listening music," he said, leaning back lazily, "and that's being told by anyone that I should stick to a dress code. It's always driven me crazy."

"Well, I know that, Cary," Jane said, pouring cream into her coffee. "But in the case of a diner, where people are ordering food, I think that some adherence to the sanitation rules should be observed."

"Maybe, but I still hate to be told how to dress."

"Oh, dear. I wonder how you're going to like what I have planned for the W.B. party, then," Jane said.

"What? You're thinking up something strange?" Cary looked indignant. "Don't forget, we're the band. We dress as Ambulance, not in whatever party theme you girls have thought up!"

"But that's just it, Cary," she said. "I was hoping that. . . ." And she told him quietly what it was she wanted the musicians to wear.

"No, no, no," Cary said vehemently. "There's no way we'd show up like that. Jane, come on, give me a break!"

But Jane smiled a serene little smile and said nothing. She was fairly certain that, in time, she could change Cary's mind.

At five o'clock that evening, the three curious residents of 407 were hiding behind some bushes outside of Addison House, the dorm next to Baker. The night was a cold one, but it hadn't turned dark yet, so the girls figured they'd be able to see when their quarry came out of Addison.

"They're sure to be in costume," Andy said to Jane and Toby. "After all, it's a costume party she's giving."

"Yes," Jane said grimly, "and I want to see what they've decided to wear."

"Do you really think we should be hiding and spying like this?" Toby asked, feeling uncomfortable about the whole thing.

"Absolutely. She's been spying on us, hasn't she?" Jane said.

"Look, the door just opened," Andy whispered. "Here they come."

Gigi and Yolanda came out the door at just that moment. The girls from 407 Baker House drew in a deep breath of horror at what they saw: Gigi and Yolanda dressed for their Come as Someone You Hate party.

Gigi Norton was wearing a red wig that looked suspiciously like Toby Houston's curly hair. She was wearing a scuzzy old pair of Western boots, a ragged flannel shirt, and a tight pair of unwashed jeans. She had a Western hat ready to plop on top of the red curls, and, what was worst of all, she was wearing a dried out old tea bag across her forehead!

"I can't believe it," Andy said, fuming. "She has the nerve to dress like Toby, but look how awful she made herself up to be!"

Toby was staring through the bushes at

Gigi. "Do I look that awful?" she asked, sounding more interested than insecure.

"Of course not!" both her roommates told her.

Andy went on, "Why, that Gigi! She ought to be thrown into a big vat of toxic waste! I just can't believe this!"

"But wait a minute," Jane said, the first to use her head a little bit. "Just because they're all dressed up for this party doesn't mean there's going to *be* a party."

"Oh, yeah," Andy said. "That's right. The fun hasn't yet begun. They're going over to Pizza Pete's, expecting guests to show up, and from the way we've heard it, nobody's going."

"So why don't we just make a few plans of our own?" Jane suggested.

"Absolutely," Andy agreed. "They can't be allowed to insult Toby like this."

The three of them went back to Baker House to conspire with their neighbors from Room 409, Maggie and Dee.

In Greenleaf, Gigi, dressed as Toby Houston, was pacing the floor in the back room of Pizza Pete's. It had been decorated for a party with balloons and crepe paper, and the tables had been set for about twenty girls.

But Gigi was becoming frantic. The Come as Someone You Hate party was supposed to have started at six, and it was now almost six-thirty. There was no one in the room except Gigi and Yolanda.

"I can't understand it," Gigi said angrily. "I put up posters everywhere, didn't I? Who could resist free pizza and sodas? And the best party idea ever to grace this dump?"

"I know, Gigi," Yolanda said mournfully. "But probably people will still show up."

Yolanda was wearing an outfit that was meant to be Ms. Merriweather, the head cook at Canby Hall's dining hall. She was all in white, even to white shoes, and she had a curly white wig that vaguely resembled the elderly, pleasant Ms. Merriweather.

Just then Gigi brightened up. Five *very* strange creatures were coming through the door. They were totally unrecognizable, but at least they were probably human beings somewhere inside the disguises.

"Welcome, welcome," Gigi trilled, hurrying toward her only guests. "Whoever you are, I'm *so* delighted to see you."

The five strange creatures mumbled something quite unintelligible. It was impossible to tell who they were or what they were supposed to be. The costumes were totally weird, with not a face showing.

"This isn't a Halloween party, you know," Gigi went on, toning down her enthusiastic welcome as she looked over the loony outfits. "You're supposed to be dressed as *people*, you know. Someone you hate."

"Oh," said a muffled voice. It was coming from inside a big glob of red and yellow material that covered the speaker's whole face and body. "We thought you said some *thing* you hate."

"No, no!" Gigi groaned theatrically. "How could you get it wrong? I specifically wrote it on all the posters I put around school. Oh, how could you?"

Yolanda touched Gigi on the shoulder. "It doesn't really matter that much, does it, Gigi? At least they came. And they can have a laugh at our costumes!"

Gigi smiled at that. "Yes, of course," she said. "Well, girls, whoever you are, why don't you guess who Yolanda and I represent?"

The five figures were silent.

"Well, then I'll tell you," Gigi went on, smugly triumphant. "My costume, as you can see, is meant to be a certain rather scruffy, and *very* rude girl at our school — "

"Toby Houston!" Yolanda finished for her. Gigi turned and gave Yolanda a dirty look.

"Quiet, Yo."

Still, the five newcomers were quietly standing there and staring at Gigi.

"Well? Aren't you hysterical, or what?" Gigi said. "It took me a long time to find all this grubby Western stuff for my costume. I expected at least a chuckle from my guests."

Total silence.

"Let me tell you who I am," Yolanda said proudly. "See this white dress and wig? See this stirring spoon? I'm Ms. Merriweather, our cook!" Yolanda began laughing all by herself, oblivious to the fact that no one else was amused. "Get it? I hate the food at Canby Hall, so I hate Ms. Merriweather! Isn't that a scream?"

But no one responded.

"This charade has gone on long enough," Gigi said abruptly. "You five are going to have to identify yourselves. Tell who you are, or what it is that you hate, if you expect to stay here and eat my pizza."

The two red and yellow blobs stepped forward. One of them spoke in a voice that was still not recognizable.

"We each represent a slice of pizza," she said bluntly. "Because that's what we really hate — pizza."

Gigi sputtered angrily. How dare they! And she thought she had heard a slight California drawl inside that big mushy slice of pizza!

But before Gigi could reply, another shapeless lump stepped forward. Her costume was white, a plain sheet thrown over her entire person. The sheet was draped with dozens of socks, all colors and types. There were sweat socks, leg warmers, bedtime socks, and even a pair of baby socks. But mostly they were real dirty sweat socks.

"I'm a sock pile," said the voice that sounded like Jane Barrett. "Rooming with you was really the pits, Gigi, but I figured the thing I hated most of all was the *socks*. And *you* remind me of dirty piles of your socks. Ugh!"

The last two girls spoke up then. They wore

brightly colored sheets that were covered with balloons and party napkins.

"We came dressed as a party because that's what we really hate — *your party*." One of the voices sounded very much like someone from a big city, one like Chicago.

The smaller one sounded like Maggie Morrison, who went on to say, "Because you're an absolute creep, Gigi Norton, to be dressed as Toby Houston like that." And she reached out to grab the tea bag from Gigi's forehead. It came off with the sticky, tearing sound of tape, pulling the red wig down over Gigi's eyes.

"Yeah, you're a creep," said all five of the guests.

"You think it's cool to be dressed as someone you hate?" demanded Andy's voice. "Well, the rest of Canby Hall doesn't think so. And that's why you're not going to see one person at this party of yours — not one!"

With that, two pizzas, one sock pile and two party collages turned and walked out.

For once in her life, Gigi Norton was unable to say a word.

CHAPTER NINE

Canby Hall remained in the grip of the freezing temperatures all that weekend. The teakettle in the Baker House kitchenette seemed always to be boiling for groups of girls wanting hot mugs of tea, coffee, clear broth, or cocoa to warm them.

"When does spring ever arrive in this crazy climate?" Toby asked on Monday afternoon as she was waiting for the teakettle to boil. She was in the kitchenette with Jane, who had just comes in from choir practice.

"You can never be sure," Jane said, stretching her legs out to keep her circulation going.

"Well, I sure would like to see some sort of signs of spring," Toby mused. "Back home, just about this time of year, we'd always start going through the seed catalogs."

"Seed catalogs?" Jane looked curious. "Your cattle ranch isn't a farm, too, is it?"

"No, no. Just cattle and horses," Toby said proudly. "But my dad always grows a big vegetable garden, come spring, so naturally we'd be interested in the catalog, to see the newest squashes and pumpkins and varieties of string beans." Toby sighed and reached for her tea mug.

"Oh, cheer up, Toby," Jane said, putting out a hand to touch her friend's shoulder. "I know you get homesick at times, but look at all the good times we have here at school."

"Oh, sure. Like I say, I'm just wishin' for some sign of spring." Toby tried to smile. "Maybe I ought to get a library book and look at some pictures of newborn calves."

"That might help," Jane said doubtfully, but then, suddenly, a big grin spread across her face. "Or something like this might help even more!"

Jane was looking over Toby's shoulder at someone who had just come in the front door of Baker House, a messenger boy from the local florist.

"Flowers for Miss October Houston," the boy said, peering into the kitchenette. "Do you ladies know who that might be?"

"We certainly do," Jane said briskly, while Toby just stood there looking absolutely dumbfounded. "Come on, Toby, take your flowers. There's your sign of spring!"

The box that Toby opened contained a large spray bouquet of daisies, daffodils, tulips, and a host of other spring blossoms. The card inside said, "Looking forward to Saturday night. Love, Neal."

"These are *beautiful*," Toby murmured, her green eyes growing wide with amazement. "Must be from a hothouse."

"Must be," Jane said with amusement. "Well, however they do them, they sure are beautiful, and you're a lucky girl, Toby Houston."

"Yes." Toby nodded, tears springing into her eyes. "We better find a vase," she said in a soft voice. "There must be one in the cupboards here."

The girls found a tall glass vase left by some long-ago student or housemother. Just as they were arranging the flowers in the vase, another delivery arrived at Baker House. By this time a crowd of girls was gathering around the kitchenette, all of them interested in Toby's flowers.

"Parcel post for Andrea Cord," called out a man's voice.

"I'll sign for that," Jane said, staring at the huge brown-wrapped box. "Well, no surprises here. It's from Chicago."

"Goodies from the Cords!" someone yelled, and even more Baker House girls appeared in the front hall to head for the kitchenette. Every girl in the dorm knew about the legendary packages of delicious food that the Cords were always sending to Andy.

"Let's have a guessing pool," Rita Martin said. "Will it be brownies or fudge?"

"Homemade oatmeal cookies or date bars?" someone else guessed. "Boy, the Cords sure do make good cookies."

So when Jane and Toby started up the stairs toward Room 407, Toby was carrying her vaseful of flowers, Jane was carrying Andy's package from home, and at least a dozen Baker House girls were trooping along behind them.

The large group of girls entered Room 407 and a startled Andy whirled around at her desk chair.

"What is *this*?" she asked, but she had a happy twinkle in her dark eyes.

"Food from home, from the Andy-sick Cords," Jane said. It was a joke around Baker House that Andy had almost never been homesick for her family, but that the Cords were continually "Andy-sick" for their girl, and hence all the food packages and telephone calls.

"Great," Andy said, stretching out her arms. "Makes for a great celebration bash. Because I have fantastic news. I am *finished* with the first draft of my history paper!"

Everyone cheered with happiness for her.

"That's superb," Jane said. Then, realizing how prim her words had sounded, she held out her hand for a joyful high five with Andy.

"All riii-iight," Toby called out, grinning like the Cheshire cat. "Things are really looking up, aren't they?" Shyly she held out her vaseful of flowers to show Andy.

"Well I guess they are," Andy said shrewdly. "Those are from Neal, I take it?"

"Yes. He wrote that he's looking forward to Saturday night!" Toby confided.

"So are we all," called out Maggie Morrison, who was perched impishly on Andy's bed, waiting for the Chicago package to be opened. "But for now, it's pig-out time. Come on, we have a bet on this package, Andy. I say it's some sort of candy."

"No, fruitcake," said Jeanne from down the hall.

"Fudge," said someone else.

Andy tore open the package as everyone gathered around. But when it was open, everyone stood back, sort of bewildered.

A note on top of the inner box said, "This is called a Survival Kit. It's to help you through the grueling work of getting your term paper ready. Stay in good health! With lots of love, Mom and Dad, Charlie, Ted, and Baby Nancy."

Inside was a strange assortment of what the Cords considered survival items. It was a nightmare.

Three bottles of organic vitamins. A box of natural prunes. Two packages of herbal tea. A bag of gorp. Some Turkish dates.

"Health food!" Andy moaned. "They should know I hate that stuff!"

"It's all probably guaranteed to make your brain work," Jane said in amusement.

"Yeah, sure." Andy went on pulling items out of the box. Beef jerky sticks for protein. Jars of saltless nuts for enegry.

"What's this? A grow-your-own-sprouts kit? Yikes!" Andy was shaking her head in despair. "Those parents of mine. They must have gotten onto a health-food kick. I mean, who needs *this*? Bars and bars of wheat germ granola?"

"They're good for you," Dee Adams pronounced, stretching out her long legs for emphasis. "We eat health foods all the time in California. And we have some of the healthiest people in the nation."

"Well, this is Massachusetts, not Laguna Beach," Andy said sadly. "It happens to be cold here, and it would have been a lot more fun to have some gooey, rich, sugary sweets."

"I agree," said Rita, who was backing away from the goody box with a horrified look on her face. Her sentiments were echoed by a few more of the Baker House girls.

"Well, so long now, Andy." One by one they were slipping out the door, having lost interest in the package from home.

"Health foods," Jane observed. "Fastest way to dampen a party, it seems." She watched as five more girls smiled politely and marched out the door.

"Well, I don't care," Maggie said. "I think

it was terrific of the Cords to send all this healthful stuff. They know that Andy still has the hardest part of her paper still to do: the revising and the final typing."

"Ugh," said Dee. "The final typing. What a job!"

The number of people in the room had dwindled down to only five now, the girls of 407 and Maggie and Dee.

"So what else have you got in there?" Dee asked with true curiosity. "Any tofu? Now that's a real treat for anyone who's looking for protein energy."

"Give me a break," Andy said, shaking her head. But just then she penetrated the final layer of the box's contents. Hidden down underneath a cardboard barrier was another whole section. The girls who had deserted the room had never suspected anything like this.

"Wow. Those people left too soon," Andy said, breathing in. "Take a look at this, folks."

"It really is a survival kit," Maggie said, her eyes widening. "The top layer was just a booby trap, to chase away the predators."

The bottom layer contained the most gooey, most high-calorie little iced cakes that any of them had ever seen. They were unbelievably beautiful.

"Petit fours," Jane said, reaching for a tiny strawberry cake and taking a bite through layers of filling. "Absolutely outrageous," Jane pronounced when she had swallowed.

The rest of them dove in.

"This makes up for all the health stuff," Andy said happily. "Thank you, dear parents. You haven't lost your sense of humor, after all."

While the rest were munching, Toby had an inspiration. She went down to the end of the hall where Laura Lee Evans had her small single room. Knocking on the door, Toby noticed that Laura Lee had the only plain door in the whole dorm. Toby had never seen one before with no message pad, no comical pictures, and no silly sayings cut out from magazines and glued to the wood.

The door was opened by a sleepy-looking Laura Lee.

"Oh, I'm sorry," Toby blurted out immediately. "You were taking a nap."

"That's all right," Laura Lee said, looking confused. "What's wrong? Is there a dorm emergency or something?"

"Oh, no," Toby said cheerfully. "We're just having a little pig-out party in our room, Room 407, you know?"

"Yes, I know where you live."

"Well. We're munching away on Andy's package from home, and I suddenly thought of you. Thought you might like to join us."

Now Laura Lee really looked puzzled. "No, thank you," she said as politely as she could. "I'm not hungry."

"You're sleepy, I suppose," Toby said quickly. "And I am sorry I disturbed you. Maybe next time?"

"Maybe," the girl said, but it was obvious from her tone that she doubted it.

"Anyway, here." Toby thrust out her fist and put something into Laura Lee's hand.

"But what?" Laura Lee seemed bewildered. She opened the little package with her slender, delicate fingers.

"That's a petit four," Toby said proudly. "At least that's what Jane calls them. Me, I'd probably just call 'em little square fancy cupcakes."

"But — "

"Just wanted you to have one," Toby said amiably. "It's an old custom back in Texas. When you have a neighbor you don't know too well, you take a cake over to them. Best way in the world to make friends."

"Friends." Laura Lee repeated the word as though she'd never heard it before. She had been staring down at the little cake, but now she raised her eyes to search Toby's face.

"Sure, friends," Toby told her. "Everyone needs friends, Laura Lee. I'm the best one to tell you that, 'cause I thought I could live here at Canby Hall and not need anybody."

"You did?" Laura Lee seemed surprised.

Toby thought the whole conversation was getting a little weird, but she kept on plugging.

"Yes. But I soon found out that life is much better when you let friendship in. We'd all like to be your friends, you know," she went doggedly on. "Jane, Andy, Maggie, Dee, and me. All you have to do is decide to accept our offer." Toby gave a little shrug, as if to show that there was no immediate pressure being put on Laura Lee.

"Well." The girl continued to stare at Toby, and suddenly there was a tiny ghost of a smile around the corners of her mouth. "Well, maybe next time then."

But this time it sounded, at least to Toby, as though maybe Laura Lee meant it.

CHAPTER TEN

Yolanda, you are such a mega-dork!"

"I am not."

Gigi Norton and Yolanda York were hiding in the narrow, dark broom closet on the fourth floor of Baker House. They had been spying all afternoon on the girls from 407 and 409.

"I learned a couple of things, Gigi," Yolanda went on.

"What?"

"Well, those girls are always trying to make friends with Laura Lee Evans. I heard them talking about it while they were sitting there eating those little cakes."

"They are? What did they say?"

"They said that pretty soon they'd get through to her."

"That's what they said, *get through* to her?" Gigi seemed intrigued. "I wonder what they want from her?"

Yolanda shrugged. There wasn't much

room in that broom closet for two, and it wasn't easy to shrug.

"To be her friends, I guess," Yolanda said.

"Never. They must have something really sleazy up their sleeves. They want something from Laura Lee. We'll find out what. Maybe we'll keep an eye on her, too."

"We will?"

"Yes! This is a serious pursuit, here. We have to do it one hundred percent right if we're going to get total revenge."

"Yeah. They were rotten to us at our party."

"*My* party," Gigi corrected her. "The whole school was rotten to us, but it's all the fault of those three from 407! Well, we'll show them."

"We will?"

"First of all, Toby's going to get a big surprise from her dear boyfriend Neal."

"But she just got those flowers from Neal!"

"Those were obviously sent before he received the letter. Just wait until that little scenario takes place."

"And then what?" Yolanda asked.

"Just you wait and see. I heard quite a few things myself, and I've got a gigantic idea in mind. It's brilliant, even if I do say so myself. It will rock them so hard that they'll all be applying for different roommates in just a few days."

"Why?" Yolanda asked.

"Oh, shush and let's get out of this scuzzy closet. You take a look. Are any of the girls out there?"

Yolanda looked. "No," she said.

The two of them slipped out of the narrow closet and came face to face with Meredith Pembroke.

"Yolanda, I'll kill you. You said no one was out here," Gigi hissed under her breath.

"No, you asked if any of the girls were out there," Yolanda said. "There were no girls out there, just Meredith."

"What's going on here?" asked Meredith, walking toward Gigi and Yolanda. "You two are not in my dorm, are you?"

"No, ma'am," Gigi said quickly. "We live in Addison."

"Well then why — " Meredith hesitated for a minute, knowing this had to be a crazy question with a crazy answer. "Why were you in the broom closet in our dorm?"

"Um . . ." Yolanda could not think of an answer.

"It's a scavenger hunt, ma'am," Gigi lied quickly. "We have to look around for brooms and mops until we find one that has green writing on the handle."

"Green writing on the handle?" Meredith opened the closet door and looked at the assortment of cleaning tools in there. "Well, these all have writing on them, but no green, I see."

"That's right," Gigi said with a shrug. "So it looks like we have to go on to Charles House, to see what they have."

"It looks that way." Meredith looked at

them strangely. She didn't believe this story for a minute, but she wasn't quite sure what she wanted to do about the situation. After all, these two hadn't broken any rule that Meredith knew about. At least not yet.

But Meredith decided that she was going to keep an eye on those two from now on. She didn't trust them, somehow.

That's an understatement, she thought, watching them as they scurried away, both giggling with relief. She didn't trust them one bit.

The first trouble started for Toby that night. She decided to call Neal and thank him for the flowers. Jane was going to the phones with her because she wanted to clue Neal in on what to wear to the W.B. party, even though it was to be a secret from Toby and Dee for now.

"So when I talk to Neal, you just leave for a little while, okay, Toby?" Jane said.

"Sure," said Toby agreeably. "I don't want to know any of the surprises yet. I won't listen."

They were able to get a pay phone downstairs and Jane dialed while Toby held the receiver.

"Hello, Neal?" Toby said eagerly. "This is Toby. October Houston. I wanted to thank you for the perfectly beautiful bouquet that you — Neal, what?"

Jane watched Toby's face become all white and pinched.

"What do you mean?" Toby gulped. "What are you talking about? What letter?"

Jane began to feel apprehensive. "What is it, Toby?"

But Toby went on listening, looking more and more confused and heartbroken by the minute.

"No, that's not true. Neal, no, she wouldn't have — "

"What's happened?" demanded Jane, really upset now.

"No, Andy would never — "

Suddenly Toby was holding a dead telephone.

"He hung up, Jane," she said in a small, miserable voice.

It took Jane a while to get the story out of Toby, because she was sobbing uncontrollably.

"I knew it was too good to be true," Toby wailed. "I knew I could never have a real date with someone as terrific as Neal. And those flowers, too. It was all like a fairy tale dream. . . ."

Jane stamped her foot. "Will you stop it, Toby Houston! You have got to tell me what Neal said!"

But Toby just sobbed louder. And hiding behind the chairs in the empty lounge in Baker House, Gigi and Yolanda were laughing quietly and enjoying every minute of Toby's misery.

"Toby, stop crying and talk to me," Jane went on insisting. Finally she was able to calm Toby down.

"Neal said he got this most awful letter!" Toby explained. "I can't believe it, but he said the letter was from Andrea Cord!"

"That's crazy. Why would Andy write to Neal?"

"He said the letter was typed and then signed with Andrea Cord's name," Toby said. "And the letter said the most terrible things."

"What sort of things?"

"Oh, that I never really wanted to ask Neal to the party at all. That I really wanted a date with the most handsome cowboy in the East, Randy Crowell."

"Oh, that's terrible," Jane said. "But we know that Andy didn't write the letter. Why would someone else?"

"That's not all," Toby said. "The letter also said that I don't like Neal at all."

"What? Well, that's not at all true!"

"Of course not." Toby had big fat teardrops running down her face. "The letter said that I was always going around making fun of Neal, saying that Neal Worthington was a big stuffed shirt and a wimp!" She began to bawl at that. "In fact, it said preppy wimp."

Jane stared at her roommate. "Well, I know how to fix this," she said briskly and dug out more change for the telephone. She called Neal immediately.

"Neal, now you listen to me, and you listen good," Jane said. "There is no way that Andy wrote that letter, and so you must realize that it was written by someone who hates us, all of us in Room 407. Agreed?"

Apparently Neal agreed with that.

"So, it stands to reason that absolutely *none* of the things in the letter is true, Neal. Now surely you can see the logic of that!"

Neal evidently did because Jane began to relax visibly.

"Now, you just talk to Toby again and apologize, Neal. What do you mean, for what? For hanging up on her, that's what! I know you were upset, but you certainly weren't brought up to do such unforgivable things as that."

Eventually Jane turned the telephone over to Toby, who had stopped crying and was just looking very subdued and unhappy.

"Hello, Neal? Yes, of course I forgive you. I understand, you were upset, and I don't blame you. But Jane is right; none of that stuff in the letter is true."

Then Jane slipped away as Toby began to talk in lower tones to Neal, and it began to sound as though Neal and Toby were getting along just fine again. Even more than fine, in fact.

Smiling, Jane went into the lounge. There she saw Laura Lee standing at the bookcases near the window. Laura Lee was thumbing through the H volume of the old encyclopedia that had been donated by some Canby Hall alumna.

"Hi there, Laura Lee," Jane said.

"Oh, hi, Jane." This time she definitely seemed friendlier than at their last encounter. "Do you know, something funny is going on around here?"

"Yes, I do know that," Jane said. "But what do *you* mean?"

"Well, I walked in here a few minutes ago and I thought I heard giggling, really muffled laughing, from behind chairs or something."

"I see," Jane said. She began to look behind the chairs herself.

"No, I tried that. But maybe whoever — or whatever — I heard sneaked away."

"Sounds like someone could have been hiding here," Jane said. She frowned, thinking hard. "Tell me, did you hear the front door open and close after that?"

Laura Lee tried to recall. "I'm not sure. I don't think I heard it. But come to think of it, there was a rush of very cold air all of a sudden."

"Just what I thought. I'll bet our sneaky gigglers were girls from another dorm, and when you came in they took off back to their own house."

"But who? And why, Jane?"

Jane hesitated. She didn't like to make accusations prematurely, but she suspected that Gigi and Yolanda had been hanging out here. And that they were the ones who had written that letter to Neal, because it was just exactly the sort of rotten thing that Gigi would do.

"It's kind of a long story, Laura Lee," Jane said. "Do you want to hear it?"

Unexpectedly, Laura Lee nodded and sat down on the edge of the old sofa. So Jane told her about the "Come as Someone You Hate" party and the whole story about the letter to Neal.

"If she did that, Gigi must be a terrible person," Laura Lee said almost in a whisper. "I didn't know anyone could be that terrible!"

"Well, I used to room with her and I think of her secretly as the Worst Person in the World."

"It's kind of scary, all this intrigue that goes on at a boarding school," Laura Lee said suddenly. "I don't think I like it at all."

"Oh no, Laura Lee," Jane protested. "It's not as bad as all that, not when you have friends who care."

"I don't know," Laura Lee said. "I don't believe I can handle it." And she jumped up and ran out of the room, leaving the encyclopedia still open on the table.

Jane went over to see what Laura Lee had been researching.

The page was turned to the HEA section of the book. Jane stared at the encyclopedia. Laura Lee could have been reading about

Health Insurance, Hearing Aids, William Randolph Hearst, or Hearts.

Maybe she's deaf, and wears a hearing aid, Jane thought. That could explain a lot of things: why Laura Lee was afraid to make friends; why she wore her long dark hair over her ears; why she was so frightened of Gigi and all her ugly tricks.

But no, that didn't seem so likely. After all, Laura Lee had heard the gigglers behind the chairs.

I don't know what her problem is, then, Jane thought, closing the book and putting it back on the shelf with the others. *But I do think we're starting to make progress with her. We're getting there.*

Right now she had more urgent things to worry about. And the most important was the trouble she was sure Gigi was trying to cause among the roommates in 407.

CHAPTER
ELEVEN

I just hope you really and truly realize, Toby, that I did not write that letter," Andy said later as the three friends, back in 407, were getting ready to go to bed.

"Of course I know it, Andy," Toby said.

"Good grief, I wouldn't have had *time* to write any crazy letters, even if I'd wanted to — which I didn't," Andy went on.

"I know," Toby said.

"That's right," Jane put in. "Andy's been working practically twenty-four hours a day on her black women in American history paper." Jane sat on her bed in her flannel nightgown with little flower bunches across the bodice. She was starting to look slightly frazzled. She'd been playing peacemaker between her two roommates for almost a week now, and it was all so silly. It was also very exhausting.

"Neal and I are friends again, so let's just forget all about it," Toby said, yanking off her cowboy boots. "It's pretty plain that whoever sent that letter hates me — a lot."

"And we know who it is who hates you," Jane said through clenched teeth.

"We do?" Toby looked surprised.

"Have you forgotten so soon?" Jane said. "Gigi Norton dressed up as you for her stupid party."

"Of course!" Andy said. "It had to be Gigi who sent the letter. But I wonder how she knows so much about our party and our boyfriends?"

"She knows a lot," Jane said. "Gigi has a real talent for snooping and spying. And she's probably gotten poor Yolanda to help her."

"Sick," Andy said, shaking her head. "Totally sick, the two of them."

"If they wrote that letter, then they're lower than a diamondback's belly, and that's pretty low," Toby pronounced.

"Lower than a paramecium on the evolutionary scale," Andy added.

Jane said, "And she may still have some more rattlesnake tricks up her sleeve."

Dearest Steve,

The reason you haven't heard from me in over a week is that I had a history paper due in a big hurry. My own fault for neglecting it until the end. Anyway, I've written a terrific paper (I think!) on black women in American history that ought to get me the A that I want for that course. All I have left to do is type the thing — it's going to be at least twenty pages long — and then I'm all set. Freedom once again!

How are things at Steak and Ribs? Are my folks still missing me as badly as ever? Are you still presiding over tables 10 through 15? And do you sometimes think of me and the way we worked so well together over Christmas vacation?

I'd like to write lots more but I'm too weary to put one more word on paper. Instead of battle fatigue, I've got paper fatigue. Please keep your letters coming, and I will write soon with a more coherent letter than this one.

> Love,
> Andy

After classes the next day, Andy went into Greenleaf to buy fresh typing supplies for her history theme.

She was feeling great this afternoon. Just having the first draft of the paper all written was the biggest relief imaginable. And her friends had offered to help her with the typing if she got too tired. She was feeling confident now that she'd hand that paper in on time.

Meanwhile, her trip to the stationery store was being impeded by all the fascinating shops along the Greenleaf streets. As a girl who loved shopping, Andy found herself stopping every minute or so to peer into store windows.

There was an awesome display of jewelry in The Jewel Box window. There in Laurel's Attic display case, she saw some really funky old dresses that had been spruced up so that she could easily imagine herself in one. And even in the Kidlet Shoppe window, she admired a display of dresses. She tried to decide which she'd buy for her baby sister Nancy if she were a millionaire looking to spend money.

But then Andy saw something even stranger than her fantasy of being a millionaire. She watched as a taxicab pulled up not two buildings away from her. The passenger in the cab was Laura Lee Evans, Andy was sure. Almost without thinking she pressed herself back out of sight into the store entrance of the Kidlet Shoppe.

Laura Lee, sure enough, but as she stepped out of the cab, Andy saw that she wasn't alone. Of all people, Michael Frank the psychologist was with her.

Andy watched, fascinated, as the Canby Hall counselor also climbed out of the taxi and handed money over to the driver.

"Now, Laura Lee, are you sure you don't mind my going upstairs with you?" Michael asked, sounding quite professional.

Laura Lee's face was as blank as a mask, showing no emotion whatsoever. "Of course not, Michael," she replied. "Because it won't make any difference, one way or another."

What is going on? Andy wondered, moving

forward just a tiny bit to hear whatever else
might be said. But she couldn't hear anything
more, and she watched, frustrated, as Michael
and Laura Lee went inside the tall modern
building.

Andy scurried over to read the sign at the
side of the door they had entered.

"Professional Building," the sign said, and
after that were listed the names of at least
twenty professional offices that were located
upstairs. Andy stared at all the names and
titles. Lawyers. Doctors. Dentists, quite a few
of them. There was even a travel agency.

Andy had not a clue as to what office
Michael and Laura Lee had gone to. And she
knew, of course, that it was none of her business, really. Whatever dealings the school
counselor and Laura Lee had in this building
were obviously confidential. Andy had no
wish to pry into someone else's private life.
She turned away and started toward the
stationery store.

She bumped right into Yolanda York.

"What are you doing here?" Yolanda demanded. "I might have known. You're following them, too!"

"What are you talking about, Yolanda?
Following who?"

"Laura Lee and Michael, that's who. Gigi
said you guys are trying to get something from
Laura Lee, and Gigi was right. You follow
Laura Lee all around, I bet."

Andy stared at Yolanda. "You're crazy," she

said firmly. "I'm not following anyone. But obviously you are. And at Gigi's orders. Well, well." Andy pretended to be amused by all this.

"What's so funny? Bet you didn't know she goes to visit Michael all the time in his office," Yolanda sniffed. "She's probably a nut case, that one."

"What a terrible thing to say!" Andy snapped. "Plenty of people go to see Michael Frank for — all sorts of things. You should never say that someone is a nut case!"

"Oh." Yolanda looked slightly ashamed of herself. Andy had the fleeting thought that maybe Yolanda wouldn't be such a total creep if she didn't hang out with Gigi.

"And it's not nice to trail around after someone, Yolanda," Andy went on. "Why don't you leave poor Laura Lee alone?"

Yolanda looked confused, then nodded triumphantly. "See, even *you* call her poor Laura Lee!" Yolanda said. "And we want to know why. What's the big mystery about her?"

"It's none of your business!" Andy burst out, even though it was true that she and her roommates were dying to know Laura Lee's secrets as well.

"So what?" Yolanda said in a taunting voice. "We know lots about her. Like, for instance, that she never takes gym class."

Andy almost said, "Is that true?" But she stopped herself just in time.

"I don't care," Andy made herself say with great scorn. "None of this is anyone's concern. Good-bye!" She didn't want to stand here on Main Street with Yolanda York for one minute more, even though she was growing more and more curious about Laura Lee.

CHAPTER TWELVE

It's looking good," Maggie declared. "Really looking good there!" Maggie was standing behind Andy's desk, staring down at the paper in Andy's electric typewriter. Andy had already reached page five of her final draft.

"You people didn't know I was such a good speed typist, did you?" Andy crowed. "Well, surprise. I happen to be a whiz on the keyboard."

"But how, Andy?" asked Jane. "You haven't taken a typing course yet, have you?"

"Nope," she said. "But when you have an older brother who needs a lot of his papers typed, you force yourself to learn."

"How nice," Toby said. "You did Charlie's papers for him?"

"Sure. That was one way to get all sorts of favors from him," Andy admitted with a big grin. "He'd drive me places after school. He'd let me play his hottest albums. He'd let me borrow his stereo. I'm not dumb, you know."

It was Wednesday afternoon, and all of Andy's friends were stopping by and offering to help. Andy, however, was having none of it. She knew she could do the typing faster by herself, and besides she'd be making last-minute changes to the term paper as she worked.

"Well, the least we can do is get you some sodas," Jane said, looking up from a magazine. She was sprawled out on her bed in the middle of her usual sort of mess — sweaters, blazers, and skirts.

"I'll go into town for food supplies," Toby offered. "I need to stretch my legs anyway — I mean my femur and tibia. Yikes. I've been studying about bones too long!" She put her jacket on.

"I'd offer to go with you," Dee said lazily from the doorway, "but I'm painting away on my palm tree. It's awesomely stunning, by the way, in case anyone cares."

"Of course we care, Dee." Maggie grinned devilishly. "As a matter of fact, you could say you have us in the *palm* of your hand."

"Oh, bad pun! You see what I have to put up with?" Dee demanded, and disappeared back to 409 and her wall painting.

"Well, I'm on my way for food reinforcements," Toby said, zipping her jacket and plopping a knitted hat on her head. "Any requests?"

"Pizza," said Maggie.

"Cherries jubilee!" Jane said in a teasing voice.

"Just go," Andy said, sounding slightly irritated. "I really can't concentrate with all this noise going on around here!"

Toby picked up her bright red mittens and tiptoed out the door. Maggie and Jane started pantomiming, pretending to shush each other in much the same way Ms. Kenworthy, the librarian, shushed the girls in the reading room.

"I wish you two would disappear also," Andy said through gritted teeth. "I could get done so much quicker if there wasn't all this noise and fooling around."

Just then the 407 telephone rang. When Jane answered it, a muffled voice on the other end said, "Emergency dorm meeting right now, up in Meredith's apartment."

"What?" Jane asked. She didn't recognize the voice, and it sounded as though someone was talking through a handkerchief, or with at least eight marbles in her mouth. "Who is this?" Jane demanded.

"Meredith wants everyone up in her apartment, right away!" the voice said, followed by a faint click.

"What is it, Jane?" asked Maggie.

"Someone with a message that we all have to go to Meredith's for a dorm meeting. Emergency, she said."

"Oh," Andy said impatiently, "now what? I don't have time for this nonsense!" But she stood up, stretching herself from head to toe. Actually it felt great to stop for a few minutes. She was totally sick of typing. "Let's go then, and get this over with." Andy snapped off her desk lamp and closed the red folder that held her typed pages. She put a paperweight down on the folder and all the research papers, just to be sure no breeze could come along to scatter her precious notes.

The three of them trooped next door and told Dee about the meeting. Dee was no more thrilled than they were; she was covered with green paint, from the kerchief covering her hair to her bare toes. But her almost-life-sized palm tree was really starting to look fantastic.

"We've never been called to any dorm meeting like this before," Maggie observed as they started up the stairs to the penthouse. "Must be something really serious!"

"Oh, yeah?" Dee asked. "Then where's the rest of the dorm? Nobody else seems to be here. And why didn't they telephone Room 409, huh?"

"That does seem strange," Jane said slowly. "I wonder what's going on?"

Andy had bounded upstairs ahead of them and was already knocking on Meredith's door.

"Doesn't look to me like there's any dorm meeting here," she said. "Are you sure you got the message right, Jane? Maybe the meeting is in the lounge?"

Jane stepped up to the landing outside

Meredith's door. "I'm not sure, because the voice was so muffled."

"This is getting weird," Maggie said when, after five or six knocks on Meredith's door, no one appeared.

"Merry is not even here," Jane finally said in exasperation. "Either the meeting is downstairs in the lounge, or there is no meeting. This whole thing must be a hoax."

The four girls stood there looking at each other. "A hoax?" Andy asked. "As in practical joke? Or as in rotten trick? As in someone who's already pulled a few rotten tricks?"

Gigi Norton was on everyone's mind, although no one spoke her name.

The thing was, *Why?* Why call them out of their rooms and send them up to the floor above?

"Unless she's planning something terrible in our rooms," Jane said quickly.

"We'd better get back down there — immediately!" Maggie said.

The four of them ran back downstairs and rushed to their respective rooms.

Dee reached her room first. "Oh no, look what's been done to my palm tree!" she howled.

They all crowded around the doorway to see. Dee's beautiful palm tree, which had been so close to being completed, was now a smeared mess of green and brown paint, like some hideous impressionist painting that no museum would ever hang. The branches were no longer branches, but vile blobs of green, and the trunk had been turned into something resembling a thick, ugly snake.

"That's the worst trick anyone has ever played," Dee said, fighting to keep back tears. She had really poured heart and soul into her palm tree painting. "It's the meanest thing I can imagine a person doing."

"Think again," Andy said from the hallway, her voice deadly calm but, for anyone who knew her, full of deadly venom. "Wait till you see what they've done to me."

They all rushed over to 407. Andy was right. The worst had been done to her.

The red folder containing her history paper was *gone*. Both copies, the first draft with all the notes, and the final, typed papers — all were gone. Except for a pair of red mittens, Andy's desk top was totally bare.

The tragedy was too great for words. The girls sank down onto the beds and the floor, silent and full of horror. Everyone knew how hard Andy had been working to write the paper.

It was a nightmare.

Finally, Maggie exploded. "Whoever did this, we'll get back at them, Andy. And we'll find the paper. We will."

"You know," Jane said, "maybe we should search this room. And then the whole dorm, if necessary. Maybe the jokester just *hid* the paper. Wouldn't that be a relief?"

They all nodded in assent and jumped up. They began a methodical search of the room, first dividing it into fourths, so they would each have a quadrant for careful scrutiny.

"If only Toby were here, we could divide it into fifths," Maggie said, overturning Jane's white wicker wastebasket. Out came hundreds of papers, but none of them had anything to do with Andy's black women in history.

"That's right. Toby went for sodas and food for a celebration," Andy said mournfully. "We were celebrating the fact that the history paper was almost done, almost out of my life."

"And now it's out of your life, all right," Jane said grimly. "But hang on, Andy. We will find it!"

Toby came back into the room at that moment, her arms full of grocery bags.

"Hey, what's going on here? What's everybody pulling the room apart for?" She set down her bags, her cheeks flushed from the cold weather outside. "I have a bagful of goodies here. Hey? What's wrong with everybody?"

"The most terrible thing has happened," Maggie said. "Someone lured us out of our rooms, and then ruined Dee's palm tree."

Toby looked stricken. She put down her grocery bag as if she felt faint. "*No!* I can't believe it!"

"And, someone stole the entire folder of Andy's paper," Jane told her. "The entire thing. Notes. First draft. Typed pages. Everything."

Toby, like the others, couldn't speak for a few minutes. She turned pale and then, slowly, a deep anger began to spread across her face.

"They can't get away with this," Toby said. "That's the worst thing I ever heard of, taking someone's research paper. And you know what? Someone stole my mittens, too. I know that's minor, compared to these other things, but I had to walk into Greenleaf with no mittens."

"Toby, what do you mean?" asked Andy. She held up a pair of bright red mittens. "Aren't these yours?"

"Yes!" Toby looked pleased. "Where did you find them?"

"Right here, on my desk," Andy said in a funny voice.

Everyone turned to look at Toby and Andy.

"They can't be here in the room," Toby said. "I lost them downstairs when I was signing out on the signout sheet. I put them down for a minute, and when I turned around they were gone."

"But they were here when we returned to the room, Toby," Andy said.

"That's impossible," Maggie said. "We saw Toby putting them on when she left here."

"Now wait a minute," Jane interjected. She held up a hand as if directing traffic. "I know it looks as if the person who stole the history paper left the mittens on the desk. But it wasn't Toby! Let's not have any accusations here."

"No accusations, Jane," Andy said in a still, quiet voice. "We all know that Toby wouldn't have played this prank. Any more than I would send that letter to Neal."

"So there you are!" Jane crowed. "Both of you are being framed, it seems to me."

"Uh-oh." A quiet little cluck came from Dee, who had been ready to close Toby's drawer after searching.

"Uh-oh what?" demanded Jane. "What is it now?"

Dee held up the object of her uh-oh. It was page five of Andy's paper, and it had been hidden under a stack of Toby's Western shirts in the drawer.

CHAPTER THIRTEEN

There was an ominous silence after Dee's discovery. Andy was staring straight at Toby, and Toby was staring right back, her conscience clear. Jane panicked.

"A frame-up, that's all it is," Jane said again. "And we know who's responsible, don't we?" When no one answered her, she pressed further: *"Don't we?"*

"Of course we do," Andy finally said. "It had to be Gigi and Yolanda. But how can we prove it, Jane?"

"And more important, how can we get that history paper back?" asked Maggie.

"Should we go to the school authorities with this?" Dee asked.

"No, I don't think it would do any good," Jane said after a short deliberation. "Gigi would only deny everything, and we might get her scared enough to destroy Andy's paper.

As it is now, we can hope that she's merely hidden it someplace."

"Someplace where we can find it!" said Toby.

"But that won't be easy." Jane was beginning to feel like a junior-grade detective. "Gigi will be keeping her room locked, I'm sure, and she'll be on the lookout for any one of us. We wouldn't even dare to show our faces in Addison, or she'd suspect something."

"All right then," Dee said. "What do we do in that case?"

"We'll bide our time," Jane began, but Andy started to wail.

"I don't *have* time," Andy reminded them. "The paper is due in just two days. Two days! What am I going to do?"

"Give us one whole day, Andy," Jane said. "If we haven't found it by tomorrow night, then you'll have to — oh, I hate to say it, but you'll have to start rewriting."

"Noooooh," Andy moaned. "Impossible."

"Hang in there," Maggie said. "We'll find a way. We'll beat Gigi at her own game, somehow."

They began to make plans.

"You all look as though something awful has happened," was the first thing Laura Lee said when she opened her door. There was concern on her face. "Please come in," she added, "and tell me what it is."

Laura Lee's room, with walls of carnation pink, a bedspread in a bright shade of raspberry, pink curtains at the window, and several deep-pink floral posters on the walls, was pleasant. The colors suited Laura Lee, Jane thought appreciatively.

"Laura Lee, we need you," Andy blurted out. "We'd never intrude on your privacy if it wasn't absolutely vital, you know that."

"Laura Lee," Toby said at the same time, "we know we have no right to ask anything of you, but you're the only person who doesn't take gym class."

Laura Lee smiled at the babble of voices. "I'm listening," she said serenely. "And I'll try to help if I can. But first you've got to slow down and tell me what the problem is!"

"I'll tell you the whole thing," Andy said in a grim voice. "But can we all sit down? This is really a gruesome story, Laura Lee."

They settled themselves on the raspberry-colored oval rug, and Andy began to talk.

When Gigi and Yolanda went over to the dining hall that evening, they weren't sure what to expect. Although they knew they hadn't been seen by anyone in Baker House that afternoon, they were still somewhat apprehensive. But they weren't prepared for what they heard in the cafeteria line.

"That's right," Andy was saying to Amy Phillips, a senior from Charles House. "I am no longer speaking to my roommate Toby."

"But why in the world, Andy?" Amy asked. "I thought you three in 407 were the best of friends."

Gigi tried to get Yo's attention, but as usual Yolanda was absorbed in her own thoughts. So Gigi said nothing, but got into line behind Andy Cord and Amy.

"I may even move out of 407," Andy was saying coldly. "After all, when a person takes her roommate's history paper — "

Amy gasped. "You're kidding! Toby did that?"

"She did," Andy affirmed. "And I can't get her to admit it, either, even though her red mittens were right there on the desk as evidence."

Gigi's eyebrows went up. She was so absorbed in the conversation that she reached out blindly for some food to put on her dinner tray. She didn't even realize that she had taken a big helping of hot dogs and sauerkraut, a dining hall super-awful special.

"Are you going to tell Meredith or P.A.?" Amy asked.

"I haven't decided yet," Andy said. "I guess it depends on whether that little sneak gives the paper back or not."

"Ohhh. What about the Winter Blahs party?" Amy asked.

Andy gave Amy what could only be described as a withering look. "You don't think I'd go to any party in *her* honor, do you? No, and neither will Dee. And maybe a lot more girls, after I tell them what's happened."

Gigi was having a hard time containing her glee. She kept her eyes down, reaching again for food and taking a tall glass of milk, which was another item she despised. But it didn't matter. She was so excited that she probably wouldn't bother to eat!

"I guess the whole party is down the drain then, hmm?" asked Amy.

"I wouldn't know," Andy said. "And by the way, Amy, would you mind if I sat with you at dinner tonight?"

"Not at all."

"Thank you. I can't stand to sit near that Texas *thief*."

As they wandered off, Gigi gave Yolanda a swift kick in the ankle.

"Ouch!" Yolanda hollered. "Why'd you do that?"

"Because! Didn't you hear?"

"Hear what?" Yolanda was pouting and rubbing her ankle.

"Didn't you hear a word of that conversation? Well, I did. And now I know my plan *worked*."

"What do you mean?" Yolanda asked.

"Come over to the table and I'll tell you all about it," Gigi said, with deep satisfaction. "I'm a genius, if I do say so myself."

But on the way to her table, Gigi was sidetracked by another conversation.

The whole dining hall seemed to be buzzing

about the rift between Toby and Andy. Toby Houston was sitting with Maggie and Jane and holding forth about how Andy Cord had played a dirty trick on *her*, instead of vice versa.

"Andrea Cord wrote a letter to my boy-friend," Toby was saying when Gigi went by the table. "She made a lot of trouble for me, let me tell you! And now she has the nerve to say that I stole her silly history paper!"

"Crazy, isn't it?" Maggie said. "Well, never fear, Toby. You'll soon get rid of her. Who wants a roommate like that anyway?"

"Yeah," Toby said. They all pretended not to notice that Gigi was lingering near their table much too long.

"And even if the whole party is canceled, I don't care," Toby went on loudly. "It'll be worth it to get rid of Ms. Big-City Cord."

Gigi sailed on toward her own table now, satisfied that she had caught the main thrust of the conversation. She had never looked happier.

"Plan A, successfully completed," Jane whispered to Toby.

"Good work, women," Maggie said. "Onward and upward to Plan B!"

Jane was the first one in creative-writing class the next day. She loved the class because she had a feeling, way down deep, that maybe someday she'd turn into a really good

writer. She also admired the teacher very
much. Lily MacArthur, a tall brunette, taught
the class in a gentle but most effective way.
It was an informal class, yet surprisingly
structured — Jane's favorite of all classes at
Canby Hall.

Today, however, she was there early because creative writing was the only class she
shared with Gigi (The Worst Person in the
World) Norton.

Sitting around in a semicircle, the thir-
teen or so students often brought up their
own topics for discussion early in the session.
Jane raised her hand today.

"I have a question, Ms. MacArthur," she
said.

"Wonderful, Jane," the teacher said. "We
love good lively class discussions. Ask away."

"Thank you." Jane stayed in her seat, but
managed to speak loudly enough for everyone in the class to hear her.

"What do you think, Ms. MacArthur, of a
situation where a person has spent a lot of
time writing a paper — weeks, even — and
then, before she can turn it in, the entire
thing is stolen?"

"Oh, my." The teacher turned ashen. "That
is a tragedy of the very worst, I am afraid. Oh,
dear. I can't think of anything more terrible
for the person who did all that writing!"

"I can't either." Jane sounded very sad.
"Now, I don't know who did this awful deed,
but all I know is that a person — a room-

mate of mine in fact — has had this misfortune."

"Oh, how tragic." Ms. MacArthur sat down, looking visibly upset. "I should think that if the perpetrator is ever caught, he or she would be in serious trouble."

"That's what I thought, too," Jane said, nodding thoughtfully. "I should think that person would be expelled from school, at the very least."

"At the very least," someone volunteered. Everyone looked properly indignant, except Gigi, who only looked bored and petulant.

"Why do we have to discuss this anyway?" demanded Gigi. "It really has nothing to do with creative writing."

"On the contrary," Lily MacArthur said. "A situation like that is the nightmare of any person who has ever done any creative writing, be it fiction or nonfiction."

"Prose or poetry," Heide Fraser added.

"Oh, yes, this is a very serious problem," the teacher emphasized. "I feel very, very sorry for the girl who has had this tragedy."

"Oh, please," Gigi scoffed. "Anybody who thinks about this has to realize — why didn't the airhead take better care of her stupid history paper? I mean, *honestly*. You don't just go waltzing out of the room and leave something that valuable on the desk." Gigi stopped. Her face was suddenly a faint shade of pink. She had said too much — far too much.

Everyone in the class was staring at her.

"Well," said Ms. MacArthur. "I suppose you're entitled to your own opinion, Gigi. But I must say you have a most peculiar outlook on life."

"You're *sick*, Gigi," a taunting voice said from the circle of students. But Gigi couldn't tell where the voice had come from.

"You have no compassion, Gigi," another girl said. "You're as bad as the person who stole that history paper."

"Yes," said Heide. "And the thief is going to find herself in a *lot* of trouble. Big time."

Gigi tried not to look nervous, but the effort showed in her sudden, restless movements.

Jane, watching closely, suppressed a little smile. She was reminded of Lady Macbeth with her guilty conscience, howling around the stage wringing her hands.

Plan B completed, Jane thought, sitting back in her seat. And now for Plan C.

CHAPTER FOURTEEN

Gym class was next for most of the Canby Hall sophomores. Today Gigi Norton was noticeably absent. The girls who noticed, because they happened to be looking for her, were Toby, Dee, and Maggie.

"Well, just as we expected. She cut class," Dee said with satisfaction. They were in the locker room, getting into their sneakers and gym clothes, but keeping a close eye on Gigi Norton's gym locker. "I guess that means Plan B worked."

"Let's hope so," Maggie said.

"Gosh, I'll really miss her in class," Toby said with a straight face. She was so convincing for a moment there that Dee and Maggie turned to stare at her, before all three of them burst out laughing.

Gigi, in the meantime, had gone straight from creative-writing class to her room in Addison House. There she was so agitated that she forgot to close the door to her room.

She crashed around angrily, sorting through the drawer of her desk, until she located her locker key.

"That Jane Barrett," she was grumbling almost under her breath. "Thinks she can make somebody nervous by babbling in front of the whole class. Well, she doesn't make *me* nervous!"

Gigi looked at the locker key in her hand. When Canby Hall students first checked in, they were each given a locker in the basement of the administration building for storing their empty suitcases, trunks, or whatever else they might not want cluttering up their rooms. It was that locker key that Gigi now shoved swiftly into her coat pocket.

When she went out of her room, she was startled to see Laura Lee Evans, standing out in the hallway. She began shaking and her heart started to pound furiously.

"What are you doing here?" Gigi demanded. "This is *not* your dorm!"

Laura Lee smiled mysteriously. "Oh, sometimes I wander around while others are at gym class. Just looking over the school, you might say."

Gigi's eyes narrowed. What is this all about?

"You never go to gym class," Gigi said accusingly.

"You've done so much spying on me, maybe you can tell me why," Laura Lee said calmly.

"I? I never spied on you! Who cares about

you?" Underneath her anger, Gigi was definitely uncomfortable. She didn't know exactly how to react.

"It's odd that you forgot to close your door, Gigi," Laura Lee said in an offhand way.

"You can't scare me!" In a burst of bravado, Gigi swept past Laura Lee, but she didn't leave the dorm. "I know you're always going for sessions with Michael Frank, the school shrink. Boy, you sure must be a real head case."

"It would seem that way," Laura Lee answered, unmoved. Gigi had expected surprise, shock, denial, and maybe, tears. But Laura remained serene. It was almost as though she'd been expecting what Gigi had said.

Gigi said angrily, "Why are you here in this dorm? Are you spying on me?"

"Now why would I be doing that?" Laura Lee said sweetly. "You have nothing to hide, have you, Gigi?"

"Of course not," Gigi snapped.

"Gosh," Laura Lee went on, "you haven't done anything unusual — unless you want to count putting that locker key in your pocket. I imagine you're going to the administration building locker room where you probably left something."

"You *were* spying!"

"Hey, it's none of my business why you're going to the locker room," Laura Lee said innocently. "Just as it's really none of *your* business why I go to see Michael, now is it?"

"Is this a threat or something?" Gigi demanded. "Or is this a bribe? Something like, you'll leave me alone if I leave you alone? Is that it?"

"Why no, Gigi." Laura looked faintly surprised. "I don't know what you're talking about. I can't even imagine, in fact."

"Get out of my way," Gigi hissed. "You're just trying to drive me crazy. Well, it won't work. You're the only one who's crazy, Laura Lee, and that's obvious because you're always going to doctors and psychologists."

With that parting shot, Gigi raced down the hall and out of Addison House.

"Good work, Laura Lee," Jane said a few minutes later as the two girls met, as planned, at the Canby Hall front gates, near the statue of the lioness and her cubs. "And thanks a million. That was first-class detective work."

"I thought so, too," Laura Lee said, smiling broadly. "I thought it was kind of fun, actually."

"So Gigi went straight for the locker key, hmmm?" Jane said. "I figured she was nervous enough, after creative-writing class, to go straight to check on Andy's history paper. I think the locker might be where she hid it."

"Sure," Laura said. "The locker would have been a much safer place than her room. But what's going to happen now? What if she goes right now and destroys the papers?"

"No problem," Jane said. "Andy is following her at the moment. We're all taking turns. My shift comes up in another hour, and then Toby's."

"But don't you all have classes?"

"Yes," Jane admitted. "We're taking a chance and cutting a few classes today. We decided that this was an emergency, and the only way to get Andy's papers back."

"You guys are really something," Laura Lee said with sudden admiration. "You really are going all out to help Andy."

Jane raised an eyebrow. "Well, of course. That's exactly what friends are for," she said pointedly.

"I think it's great," Laura Lee said.

Jane put a hand on the girl's shoulder. "You did a great thing, too, Laura Lee, keeping an eye on Gigi like that. You're the only one who could have gone to Addison and confronted her in just that way, and we're all grateful to you — "

Jane was interrupted by Laura Lee letting out a strangled cry.

"My gosh, what's wrong?" Jane asked.

"Look! That car coming through the entrance gates!" Laura Lee said.

"Yes. A green Ford. Why does it upset you so much?" Jane asked.

"It's my *parents*!" Laura Lee gasped. "They make surprise visits like this sometimes. They like to find out what I'm doing, so they never let me know when they're coming."

"Oh," Jane said. "You don't really like to see them, or what?"

"No, I don't." Laura Lee was frantically smoothing down her hair. "They're always upset because I'm not — " She stopped in midsentence.

"You're not what?" Jane asked. "Come on, Laura Lee, you can tell me. I won't repeat it to anyone, I promise. Maybe I can help."

The girl looked at Jane for a long moment before she spoke. "Yes, maybe you can help this one time. But I hate to ask it."

"Ask, please. Look at the favor you did for us!"

"Well, my parents want me to mix with people here at school," Laura Lee admitted. "All the doctors want me to get involved in school life and be active in things. And most especially to have friends."

"Oh, I see," Jane said, though she didn't understand at all. What was that about "all the doctors"?

"You see, every time my parents come to visit, they find me all alone," Laura Lee went on. "And they get angry with me, and scold and fuss. Because I don't have any friends, as you know."

Jane's face took on a determined look. "Well, that's not true anymore. You do have friends now!" she declared.

The green car had been cruising slowly around the circular drive that visitors had to take to reach the main part of the campus.

Now the car slowed at the statue of the lioness and came to a halt. Laura Lee's parents had spotted their daughter.

Andy Cord was traveling from tree to tree, hiding behind each one, in pursuit of Gigi Norton. She was freezing, but she knew this surveillance mission was absolutely necessary.

Gigi, however, was simply pacing around the campus, looking nervous as a cat and uncertain of where she was going. Andy had expected something like that, though, because she knew that Plan C had involved Laura Lee being outside Gigi's room during gym class. They had all counted on Gigi being confused at this point.

Finally, after about ten minutes of the pacing, Gigi went into the library and sat down at a table with a sulky expression. Andy followed her in there, but found a stack of books where she could hide. She peered through and kept her quarry in sight, and felt quite pleased with her expertise in detective work. She guessed she hadn't watched all those *Cagney and Lacey* shows for nothing!

But what Andy didn't know was that someone was watching *her*. It was Merry Pembroke, her housemother, and Merry was perfectly aware that Andy was supposed to be in class this period.

Now what's going on? Meredith thought. *Andrea Cord — cutting a class?* She stayed hidden herself and watched as Andy Cord did some very mysterious things, such as peering through the library shelves at — who was that?

Gigi Norton. Meredith started to put two and two together. Andy was keeping an eye on Gigi Norton.

Meredith had heard through the grapevine that someone had stolen Andy's history paper. She hadn't gone to Room 407 because she'd been waiting for Andy to come to her to report the theft.

Now she continued to watch Andy but she stayed where she was. There would be time enough later to find out what exactly Andy was up to.

CHAPTER FIFTEEN

Mr. and Mrs. Evans stepped out of the green Ford, smiling with great excitement. Jane found herself stiffening; she was already prejudiced against Laura Lee's parents.

She couldn't help it. She was picturing Laura Lee's parents as some kind of monsters. After all, look how nervous the girl was: afraid of her own shadow, afraid to make friends. Somehow those parents of hers must be to blame for all that.

And then, these surprise visits of theirs! Jane bristled even more as the pair came closer to embrace their daughter. What was the meaning of their surprise visits? Only to scold and humiliate Laura Lee, as far as Jane could figure out.

They sounded inhuman.

"Hi there, darling," Mrs. Evans was saying. She was an attractive small woman, with fair skin like her daughter's and neat black hair.

Funny, she didn't sound like a severe, overly critical mother. Maybe she was more the quiet, but deadly type. She had obviously forced her poor daughter into going to boarding school, something that Laura Lee had not been ready for.

"Hi, Mom and Dad," Laura Lee said. "It's lovely to see you."

"Well," her father boomed out, sounding hearty and sincere. "We thought we'd surprise you, Laura dear, as we usually do!" He was a big man, sort of balding, with warm brown eyes.

"How nice," Laura Lee managed to say. "Well, I guess you can see that this time you surprised me, visiting with a friend."

"Yes!" Mrs. Evans turned happily toward Jane.

"I'm Jane Barrett," Jane said. She was feeling puzzled. She'd expected not to like these people at all, and instead she found herself smiling warmly at both of them.

"Don't tell me! You're one of the Barretts from Boston?" asked Mrs. Evans.

"Yes," Jane admitted.

"What a coincidence. I know your family well, Jane. You see, I was a Canby Hall girl myself, and there has often been a Barrett of Boston here at this school, even as far back as my mother's day."

"Is that right?" Jane was intrigued. "Maybe you went to school with my Aunt Cecilia? Or my Aunt Iris?"

"I certainly did," Mrs. Evans said. Her eyes were twinkling mischievously. "You just say hello to both of them for me. Tell them it's a hello from Dolly Packard, now Dolly Evans, one of The Renegade Brigade."

The Renegade Brigade?

Jane nodded, puzzled. "Hello from Dolly Packard, one of The Renegade Brigade? What does that mean?"

"That, my dear, was a secret organization we had back in the old days," Dolly Packard Evans confessed. "We used to get into more mischief than any other bunch of girls who ever attended this school."

"There were eight of them, all dedicated to making trouble, you see," Laura Lee explained. "They must have been a wild and crazy group, from what I've always heard."

Jane smiled. Imagine that. She'd never heard of such things from her aunts, but then they were such proper Bostonians that they'd never tell tales out of school.

"Sounds like fun," Jane said. She suddenly realized that she actually liked Laura Lee's mother. But how could she help it? Mrs. Evans was full of energy and high spirits.

"I'm so glad you've begun to make friends at last, Laura," said Mrs. Evans. "And imagine, a niece of my two old friends. Well, I've always told you, Canby Hall is the place to make friends."

"What are you girls up to?" asked Mr. Evans. "We thought maybe we could take you out to dinner or something. We'd love to have you join us, Jane."

"Oh, we're still in the middle of afternoon classes," Laura Lee said quickly. "We both have to get back to — to biology."

"I'm afraid that's true," Jane said regretfully. She was beginning to wish she could have dinner with the Evanses, but the first thing on her priority list had to be getting Andy's history paper back.

"Very well, don't let us stop you, girls," said Mrs. Evans. "We'll probably go and have a little chat with your headmistress. And we'll find you later, when classes are over. Perhaps then you'll consider dining with us, Jane."

"If I can," Jane said honestly. Right now she had to find Andy and relieve her on the Gigi-watching detail.

"See you later, girls." The Evanses got back into their car and drove off toward Patrice Allardyce's office.

"Thank you, Jane," Laura Lee said. "Thanks for pretending to be my friend. You really made a hit with my folks. I've never seen them so happy."

"There's nothing to thank me for," Jane said. "I didn't have to pretend. I hope we *are* friends, Laura Lee. And you know what? Your parents aren't so bad. I liked them."

"Good." Laura Lee looked a little sad, suddenly, but she started walking briskly toward the science building. "I really do have biology next. See you later, Jane."

Jane stood there for a moment, feeling bewildered. What was it with Laura Lee? One minute you could feel close to her, and then the next minute she was totally withdrawn.

Oh, well, Laura Lee had helped them with Plan C, and that was what really counted at the moment. And now it was time for Plan D.

This has got to work, Jane thought, crossing two fingers tightly. Somehow they just had to find out where Gigi had hidden Andy's history paper.

Jane was walking along one of the paths around the library, searching for Andy, when she heard footsteps behind her.

Just like in some mystery movie, she thought, and then laughed at herself. It was broad daylight! She stopped short and waited to see who was walking along behind her.

Meredith Pembroke stepped out from behind a pine tree.

"So. I see another of my girls has cut a class," Meredith said, but she didn't sound angry. She seemed to be amused.

"Oh, Merry, I can explain." But Jane knew she couldn't explain, not really. The girls had decided not to bring the school authorities in on this problem yet.

"You don't have to explain, Jane," Meredith said. "At least not at the moment. I think I have some idea of what's happening around here."

"You do?"

"I think so," Meredith said. "And I'll stay out of it for now. The only thing I'll say is that your roommate is hiding out in the library, playing detective for all she's worth."

"Oh, the library? That's where Andy is?" Jane had been wondering how to find Gigi and Andy.

"That's where she is, and so is her victim — or is it suspect?"

Jane tried to guess, from the expression on Meredith's face, just how much the housemother knew. But it was impossible. Meredith had one of those faces that could remain impassive.

"Well, thanks for being understanding, Merry," Jane said gratefully. "I guess you realize that what we're doing is super-important."

Meredith simply nodded her head. "Good luck," she said quietly. "And let me know if I can help." Then she walked off.

"Things are about to happen, I think," Andy whispered when Jane found her in the library. "Gigi looks so nervous I think she's going to start chewing her fingernails — and you knew what a fanatic Gigi is about her perfect fingernails!"

"Good." Jane peered through Andy's little peephole in the book stacks. "Maybe she's about ready to make her move."

"I wouldn't be surprised," Andy said in a low voice.

"Well look, it's my turn to watch her," Jane said. "But here's what I want you to do next."

Andy listened, her eyes widening, and then she hurried off. She left the library and headed toward the gymnasium. Just then the bell rang, signaling the end of the class period. Jane was left alone to watch The Worst Person in the World.

Gigi, looking wild-eyed and indecisive, stood up. She reached into her pocket for the locker key. She stared at it for a few minutes. Jane held her breath, watching and waiting.

Then, tossing her mane of black hair, Gigi stalked out of the library. She didn't head for the science building where she should have been in biology class.

No, she was marching straight toward the administration building where the lockers were in the basement.

CHAPTER SIXTEEN

Plan D was not looking good. Gigi was moving too rapidly, crisscrossing the campus toward Old Main, the administration building. Jane could keep up with her, but she was beginning to wonder how she was going to handle things all alone when the final showdown came.

Maybe she should have dragged Meredith along with her, or at least Andy. Maybe this was too big a problem to be tackled without the school authorities. Maybe Gigi would succeed in ripping up Andy's history papers.

Stop it, Jane, she told herself, squaring her shoulders and hurrying along after the athletic Gigi. *Whatever happens, you can handle it — because you have to!*

But that was easier said than done. When Gigi went quickly down the stairs to the basement of Old Main, Jane followed quietly. The place was cold, dimly lit, and smelled sort of musty. It seemed totally isolated from the rest of the world. Jane shivered more from a feeling of dread than anything else.

She found herself a hiding place and stepped back into shadows where she could watch Gigi. Sure enough, The Worst Person in the World went right to her locker and opened it with the key.

Jane squinted in the dim light to see what Gigi was pulling out of the locker. It looked like a folder, all right, and it was bright red — just as Andy's had been!

This was it. And nobody else was here.

"All right, Gigi," Jane called out angrily. "This is the end of the line for you. You'd better listen to me. Hand over that folder right now."

Gigi looked surprised, but not really fazed by Jane's presence.

"No, I think *you'd* better listen to me. And stand back," Gigi said smoothly. "Or else, if you take one step further, I'll start ripping these pages into shreds."

That stopped Jane dead in her tracks. "You wouldn't dare," she said, but her voice was uncertain.

"Oh, yes I would," Gigi taunted.

"Gigi," Jane ventured. "You've already been a thief. That's about as low as a person can be. And now if you destroy Andy's history paper, we'll go straight to Ms. Allardyce with this story."

"I think not," Gigi said. "It'll be just your word against mine, Jane, and there will be absolutely no evidence to show." Gigi's face twisted into a smirk and she began to tear, slowly, slowly, slowly. Jane's heart sank. Gigi was ripping the paper in her hands!

"Think again, Gigi," said an unexpected voice from the shadows of the locker room. Jane turned with surprise at the same time Gigi swiveled her head.

"That's right. There's another witness to what you're doing," said the voice. Jane knew by now that it belonged to Laura Lee Evans, but she couldn't believe it. Hadn't she seen Laura Lee go off to biology class a while ago?

Laura Lee stepped out of the shadows. "Hi, Jane. I decided to take a chance and cut a class myself. I had a feeling you might need some help over here with this — this — alleged human being."

"Oh," Jane said, breathing a sigh of relief. "I'm so glad you did! I've never been so glad to see anyone!"

Gigi had stopped tearing, but she still held the folder. They didn't have Andy's paper back yet.

"Who's going to take *your* word for anything?" Gigi taunted. "You're a fleabrained mental case, everyone knows that. Or they soon will, when I tell them everything I know!"

"Stop right there," shouted Maggie Morrison, leading four more girls at top speed down the basement stairs. She had her camera in hand and she snapped a picture of Gigi with the folder.

"You've had it, Gigi," declared Dee Adams. She rushed into the basement room with an open paint can and the paintbrush, which was dripping with green enamel paint. "You rip Andy's paper and you're going to be wearing green paint for the rest of the semester!"

Toby was carrying a Western-style rope in the shape of a lariat. "I can rope a steer in two seconds flat," Toby said in an exaggerated Texan drawl. "So I can sure rope one puny little thief like you, Gigi, if need be."

Gigi stopped, shocked by the number of girls who had arrived. She knew she was really caught red-handed now.

Maggie snapped another picture and chuckled. "I'm going to call this one, 'Study of Stupid Expression on Nasty Face.'"

Andy Cord stepped forward to the front of the group. "I'll take that folder now, Gigi," she said coldly. "I believe it belongs to me."

Gigi didn't move as Andy yanked the folder away from her. Andy looked at it quickly and was satisfied that it was her history paper. All the notes, all the pages of the first draft, and all the pages that she had typed. Luckily, the ripped pages weren't terribly damaged. They could be retyped.

"Thank you so much," Andy said sarcastically.

Gigi held her head high. "Oh, why don't you all just lighten up?" she said. "This was a joke. A prank. I was planning to return the paper to Andy."

"*Sure* you were," Dee and Maggie said in unison.

"Don't insult our intelligence," Jane flung at Gigi. "You came down here to get rid of that folder once and for all."

"Ridiculous," Gigi said. "I did not, and you can't prove a thing."

"I wouldn't be so sure," Jane went on. "Our housemother seems to know quite a lot about this whole matter. Maybe we should compare facts with her."

"No!" Gigi cried out before she could stop herself. She was remembering how Meredith had caught Yolanda and her in the broom closet.

"Oh, let's just get out of here," Andy said, turning to her friends. "Now that I've got my folder back, that's all that matters."

"Can't I just paint her face and hair a little?" Dee asked, moving toward Gigi with the brush. "Just a nice shade of Tropical Palm Tree Green?"

"It *would* be an improvement over her usual face," Maggie said, giggling.

"Let's go," Toby said wisely. "We'll find another way to teach her a lesson."

"You will not," Gigi called out as the girls were filing out of the basement room. "You're all such goody-goodies that you'll never come up with an idea."

The girls smiled. They had implemented all their strategy through Plan D, the one to have everyone assembled in the locker room to help Jane.

And now it remained only to think of a Plan E, which would be the Getting Even Plan.

Outside Andy suddenly shouted, whirling around, "Wheee! I've got my paper back! I feel like dancing."

Andy looked at the face of each girl. "Did I tell you guys yet how absolutely wonderful you all are, helping me out this way?"

"You probably did," Toby told her with a big grin. "But tell us again."

"I love you all — every one of you," Andy said as she linked arms with Laura Lee and Dee, who were the two girls closest to her. They in turn linked arms with Toby, Maggie, and Jane. Thus, arm in arm, the six of them paraded triumphantly along the campus path.

"What a team we make," Maggie crowed, doing a high step like a drum majorette. "The Invincible Six."

"We could call ourselves The Renegade Brigade," Jane remarked, smiling mysteriously at Laura Lee.

Just then, Mr. and Mrs. Evans came around the corner from Ms. Allardyce's office.

"Well, look at that, Dolly," said Laura Lee's father when he saw the six friends arm in arm. The happiness in his voice was obvious. His face was beaming with pleasure, too.

"Looks just like the old Renegade Brigade

to me," said Dolly Evans. "How wonderful. Just what we always hoped for Laura Lee."

And then suddenly Mrs. Evans did an amazing thing. She stopped right where she was, pulled out a wad of Kleenex tissues, and began to cry — softly and with happiness.

Jane was the only one who knew who the pair was and why they were being so emotional. And she was too surprised to say a word.

"Everyone," Laura Lee said, rather embarrassed. "These people are my parents. And they're going crazy because they think I have lots of friends."

"You do," said Toby quickly.

"Of *course* you do!" Maggie stated.

"Friends to the end," said Andy.

"And no doubt about it!" That was Dee.

Jane smiled. She still wished she understood all the secrets of Laura Lee's mysterious ways, but she knew it didn't really matter. Their new friend had proven herself to be a great ally, and she was one of them for as long as she wished to be.

"Laura Lee, I told you. This is no pretense," Jane said. "We really are your friends."

Mrs. Evans stopped crying as everyone introduced herself. Each girl was warm and polite and said something extra nice about Laura Lee.

It was a beautiful moment, one of those

glittering moments to be etched in stone to last forever. The girls were still arm in arm, feeling warm and caring.

"Well, isn't this simply adorable, and *so* cozy?" Gigi's voice ruined their beautiful moment. "And who might these people be?"

"We are Laura Lee's parents," said Mrs. Evans, smiling. "Are you one of Laura Lee's friends also?"

"No," Gigi said haughtily. "Frankly, she's too strange to have friends."

There was a sharp intake of breath from all six of the outraged Baker House girls.

"Gigi, I warn you — " said Andy.

"Oh, you don't warn anyone," Gigi said angrily. She still wanted revenge on *someone*. "I think the Evanses ought to know what a sicko their daughter is."

"Sicko?" asked Mr. Evans, his face darkening.

"Right. Bonkers. Froot Loops." Gigi waved her arms around dramatically. "In other words, your little Laura Lee is always running off to doctors and shrinks.

Mrs. Evans threw back her shoulders angrily. "Just a moment, young lady!"

"My parents know all about what's wrong with me," Laura Lee cut in, her voice was trembling.

Jane protested, "Laura Lee, you don't have to — "

But Laura Lee put up her hand. "I don't

have anything to hide," she said. "Not any more, not now that I have you guys for friends. The truth is, I've been avoiding people all this time and visiting Michael Frank and not going to gym class because, well, because I have a very bad heart."

CHAPTER
SEVENTEEN

A shocked silence came over the whole group. Gigi said with real nervousness, "A bad heart! I don't want to hear about this."

"A *very* bad heart," Laura Lee repeated as Gigi ran off down the path.

The rest of them stood there as still as statues and just as quiet. They were looking at Laura Lee Evans in a new way: her white porcelain skin — was that a sign of poor circulation? Her fear of people, parties, and friendships? Was that all part of having a bad heart? The naps Laura Lee was always taking and the many visits to doctors? The girls were silent, adding up all these clues.

"What you've said is simply not true, Laura Lee," said Mrs. Evans with just as much forcefulness as her daughter had used.

"Oh, yes it is, Mother!"

"No." Mrs. Evans stepped forward. "I'm glad you brought this up in front of all your friends, because I want to set the record straight, once and for all."

"No, Mother, there's nothing to set straight."

"Yes, there is, Laura Lee," said her father in a gruff voice. He looked earnestly at the group of girls. "No matter what Laura Lee tells you, she doesn't have a bad heart anymore. She has been cured. She is well now, and it only remains for her to accept that fact."

The look of confusion on all the girls' faces was evident.

Mrs. Evans spoke again. "Our girl did once have a congenital heart defect," she said. "Congenital — that means she was born with the problem. And it was a serious one."

"Oh, please, Mother, nobody wants to hear this," Laura Lee protested.

"You brought it up, dear," Mrs. Evans said. "Now, Laura Lee has had several operations to correct her condition. And the last one, a year ago, was the final one."

"It was one hundred percent successful," said Mr. Evans. "The doctors now want our girl to live a full, active, normal life."

"But that's wonderful, Laura Lee," Jane said warmly. "It's like being born all over again."

"Except that Laura Lee is afraid to leap into life," said Mrs. Evans sadly. "And that's one of the reasons that we made sure she came here to Canby Hall. Because I know, from personal experience, that every girl gets involved in good times here at this school."

"Except me," Laura Lee said glumly.

"Well, you're involved in things now," Toby said with enthusiasm. "You did all that fantastic detective work for us, and you're coming to our W.B. party and all sorts of things!"

"Are you, Laura Lee?" Mrs. Evans looked as though she was ready to cry again. "A party? That would be wonderful for you! And here you are with all these fine friends."

"I don't know about the party, Mother."

"She'll go," Andy said, clamping a hand on Laura Lee's shoulder. "We won't let her stay hidden away in her room anymore. Not now, when we know what the real story is."

"You guys, you think it's so simple," Laura Lee protested, but she looked flattered and pleased by all the attention.

"Don't worry, Mr. and Mrs. Evans," Dee said. "We're going to make sure that Laura Lee joins us in all sorts of fun stuff. I may even enlist her help in repainting my palm tree!"

"I don't know," Laura Lee said. "Everyone's been trying to get me to change my attitude. Michael Frank and all the doctors at the hospital, and even the cardiologist in Greenleaf."

Andy remembered the day she'd seen Michael and Laura Lee going upstairs in the Greenleaf Professional Building. So that was it. Michael had wanted to confer with Laura

Lee's medical doctor, maybe about Laura Lee's actual physical condition. It was all so simple when you knew the facts.

"Please just say you'll *try,* dear," begged Laura Lee's mother. "With the help of all your friends, I'm sure you'll soon feel quite at ease. You'll be going to gym class and who knows what else?"

"Swimming?" suggested Maggie.

"Ice skating even," said Toby, rolling her eyes at the memory of her own terrible experiment on the ice.

"California surfing, eventually," said Dee. "Why not? If the doctors say you're cured, then you can come out to Laguna Beach with me. You can do anything!"

"And any time I need a detective," Andy said, "I know just who to call. You were superb, Laura Lee."

Jane just smiled. She could tell that Laura Lee was listening to everything with an open mind. In time, Jane was sure, Laura Lee would be trying anything that the rest of the Canby Hall girls did.

"This calls for a real celebration," said Mr. Evans. "I'd like to invite each and every one of you out tonight. We'll have a lovely dinner at the Greenleaf Inn, if your housemother will allow it."

"And we have lots to celebrate!" Jane declared, looking at the history papers in Andy's hands.

"Yeah, but I've still got the final typing to do," Andy said, and then she smiled. "Aaaah. What the heck. I'm a speed typist. I can get the paper done in just a few hours tonight."

The girls went looking for their house-mother and finally found Merry on the steps outside Baker House. They explained about their invitation to dinner with Laura Lee's parents, and how much it would mean to the Evans family if they could all go to the Green-leaf Inn.

Merry looked right at Andy, who was clutching the red folder as if it were the Lost Treasure of the Incas.

"I see you've recovered a certain some-thing," Merry said. Andy nodded with joy.

"I'm awfully glad," Merry said. "And I guess I won't ask a bunch of questions — this time. But I hope I never have to find out that my girls are cutting classes again."

"Oh, *no*," they all promised with solemn faces.

"Good. Then we'll just have to assume it was all for a very, very good cause." Merry smiled. "And permission is hereby granted for you to dine with Mr. and Mrs. Evans."

"Oh, thank you, Merry," Toby sang out. "You've saved us from a fate worse than death!"

"What fate worse than death?"

"Eating in the dining hall, of course," Andy chimed in.

CHAPTER EIGHTEEN

Ironically, the Saturday of the Winter Blahs party turned out to be the first day of the official spring thaw.

"What happened?" Toby asked in great surprise that morning, staring out from 407's window seat. "Where did winter go?"

Everything was thawing. The temperature soared up and the trees lost their heavy burden of snow. All traces of ice were melting from the walks, and the sunshine was sparkling on actual patches of grass here and there, instead of snow.

The air smelled like spring, Toby thought, even if it was totally deceptive. All that remained was for a red robin to appear at the birdhouse on the front lawn.

"Isn't this a bummer?" demanded Jane. "Maggie and I worked so hard on this party to get rid of the Winter Blahs, and what happens? The thaw arrives."

"Doesn't matter in the least," Andy told her. "It's wall-to-wall mud outside, and that's hardly an improvement over snow. We still need the party, and bad. It's been a rough couple of weeks for me, I'll tell you."

"Yes." Jane smiled. "But at least your paper is all done and turned in on time." Jane stopped to stare at her. "It *is*, isn't it? There haven't been any more tragedies?"

"No, no," Andy said with a laugh. Hands on hips, she stood looking in the closet at all her bright party outfits. "What kind of clothes will we be wearing to this party tonight?" she asked.

"Well, don't tell Toby or Dee, but — " And Jane whispered instructions to Andy, who laughed good and loud. Then she began to assemble her party clothes.

Neal arrived early in the afternoon by train. Toby — a very nervous Toby — went to meet him at the little white depot in Greenleaf. She needn't have been nervous. When they arrived at Canby Hall, they were holding hands and swinging their arms happily, like two best friends.

Toby looked very pretty that day. Jane and Andy had trimmed and shaped her hair so that it fell into soft, gentle waves. Her cheeks were unusually pink from walking to town in the balmy weather. She was wearing a brand new oversized sweater of a soft cream color and light brown slacks, instead of her usual gray sweat shirt and Western jeans.

"She sure looks better than she did last week," Andy commented, watching Toby and Neal as they lingered outside Baker House. "Remember? When she was so sick of winter she thought she had the flu?"

"Yes," Jane agreed. "I think just the idea of the W.B. party has kept her going. Well! Are we going to make that lounge ready for the big event, or what?"

The party committee, which included Laura Lee, went to work.

Finally, it was time. Andy escorted Toby and Dee, as the official guests of honor, from the dorm's kitchenette into the lounge. They were wearing blindfolds.

"When you hear the music," Andy told them, "then you can take off your blindfolds."

"Do you hear music yet?" Toby asked Dee.

"Mmmm. Not yet." But just then, there was a loud burst of Ambulance music. It was not their usual rock and roll. This music sounded sort of tropical with a reggae beat.

Toby and Dee whipped off their blindfolds. They stared in amazement at what had been done to Baker House's lounge.

Under at least a dozen bright clamp-lamps, the place was a kaleidoscope of color, music, and confusion.

The floor of the entire huge room was covered with little white Styrofoam packing "peanuts" used for fragile packages. It was piled at least three inches high from wall to wall. It was absolutely eerie to see the rug gone, buried underneath the white peanuts.

"Welcome to our W.B. party," Jane greeted. "Our official Baker House First Annual Beach Party!"

"Beach party?" repeated Toby, with big, round eyes.

Every person there was dressed in beach clothes: Jams, loud Hawaiian shirts, and a variety of bathing suits. A pair of sunglasses sat on every nose above a white coating of zinc oxide. Flip-flops adorned every pair of feet.

Some of the boys from Oakley Prep sported the most outrageous beach hats ever seen. Eddie, Dee's date, had had a wild hat collection he'd been saving up for just such an occasion as this. So above the sunglasses and zinc-oxide-white noses, there were straw hats, sun visors, miner's helmets, Mexican sombreros, berets, safari helmets, and a raccoon skin hat. Then there was Eddie's own special hat, an ingenious creation made to hold two cans of soda with two long tubes to serve as straws to the mouth. Eddie waved at the girls as he slurped both root beer and Cherry Coke at the same time.

"This looks like a convention of West Coast nonconformists!" Dee declared gleefully. "And it sure does make me feel at home!"

"But why the stuff on the floor?" asked Toby, moving her feet tentatively in the thick layer of peanuts. They made a strange, loud, crinkling sound as she moved.

"It's our make-believe sand, of course," Jane explained. "That's the whole point. We're having a beach party. We've turned our lounge into a strip of Cape Cod."

"Yeah," Maggie said. "What better way to cure the blahs?"

Neal stepped forward with a Hawaiian lei and draped it around Toby's neck. He, too, looked outrageous in a loud jungle-print shirt and a pair of garish striped bathing trunks, totally out of character for the conservative Cornelius Worthington III.

Several cardboard hot dog and ice cream stands hung on the walls. There were bright yellow sun rays beaming down from the ceiling. And someone (Maggie) had drawn a poster of Dee on a surfboard, with a tall palm tree in the distance. Everyone was laughing at the astounded expressions on Toby's and Dee's faces.

"This is unreal, you guys," Dee announced, laughing. She plopped down into the "sand" as if she were ready for sunbathing. "Now where's my bikini?"

Maggie handed her a beach towel and beach robe. Someone else gave her a big pair of wacky sunshades. Eddie presented her with a hat that only Dee could love, with little plastic palm trees sticking up all over.

"And here's your suntan lotion, Toby," said Neal, dabbing Toby's nose with the white cream. "And a hula skirt because this group voted that the guests of honor should do the hula for us, Texas style *and* California style!"

"Oh, no," Toby groaned. But she seemed to be laughing at the idea. "This is unbelievable," she said. "Look at the guys in Ambulance."

The band members had forsaken their usual cool clothes. Instead of leather jackets and black Levis and fierce earrings, the boys were dressed like everyone else. They had the same Jams and clashing beach shirts, and white noses. And they were smiling as though they didn't really mind all that much!

"And have you seen our chaperone?" asked Jane, and Toby and Dee looked around the room. Merry was sprawled out on a beach blanket under a bright light, with a picnic cooler beside her and a big paperback book to read. The old-time bathing suit she wore was one that must have come from Laurel's Attic. It was woolen and black and covered most of her legs, arms, and chest.

"Cheerio," Merry said, smiling. "I'm all set to stretch out on the beach and get a good tan."

CHAPTER NINETEEN

"Having a good time, Laura Lee?" Jane joined Laura Lee, who was distributing cold soda from several picnic coolers placed in the "sand."

"Yes, I am," Laura Lee said. She was wearing a sun visor and a pair of striped sunglasses. "I never knew that parties could be so much fun, Jane. I'm glad I came to this one."

"We are, too, Laura Lee. You know, we feel as if you're an honorary member of 407 now."

"That makes me feel so good, you can't imagine," Laura Lee said quietly. "I just didn't realize that friendship could be so important."

"We all need people," Jane said. "Even The Worst Person in the World."

Laura Lee chuckled at that and handed several more cans of soda to members of Ambulance.

"You don't have to work at this party, you

know," Jane said. "I mean, people can help themselves to sodas. Why don't you mingle?"

"I already have mingled," Laura Lee said with a mysterious smile. And then Jane realized that Laura Lee was not alone. She was being helped with the sodas by a short, tousled-haired boy who'd come over from Oakley Prep with Matt and Cary.

"Um, Jane, this is Philip," Laure Lee said. "We met a little while ago over near that sand dune. He says he's going to teach me to dance."

Jane's blue eyes twinkled. "Well, all right!" she told them. "Got any requests? I've got some influence with the band!"

Laughing, Laura Lee and Philip went to join the dancers.

"Go, girl, *go!*" Andy called out encouragingly to Laura Lee.

"This is fun," Laura Lee called back to Andy. "I'm going to have to learn *all* the wild dances!"

Jane danced over to where Toby and Neal were.

"Everything okay over here?" she asked.

"Absolutely," Toby said happily. "This is one terrific party, Jane, and I really do thank you for it. You worked hard to make things so great."

"You're very welcome, October," Jane said with a mock primness. "It was worth it to see that smile on your face again."

"Dee looks pretty happy, too," Toby said,

pointing toward the California girl. Dee was whirling around in her beach robe and her palm tree hat, having a really great time with Eddie.

"I guess there are no Winter Blahs around here anymore," Jane said. She headed then for the one spot that meant a lot to her: right beside Cary Slade.

Cary and his group finished playing "California Girls" and called a break for themselves.

"Nice work, guys," Jane told them.

Cary put an arm around her. "This whole thing worked out better than I ever would have thought," he admitted. "I never expected the band to go for the beach clothes, but everyone seems to be having a great time."

"Well, you look awful cute with that suntan stuff on your nose," Jane teased, putting a forefinger up to touch Cary's nice straight nose.

"So do you, Jane Barrett." Cary spoke quietly so that only Jane could hear. "You're pretty special to me, do you know that?"

Jane was surprised at the unexpected warmth of Cary's words.

"Wait a minute," Cary said as their faces drew closer together. "These big sunglasses can be a safety hazard."

Jane promptly removed hers. Cary followed suit, and they shared a warm, sweet kiss.

"Hey, that's enough of *that*," called out Andy in a teasing voice. She and Matt were arm in arm, looking totally happy and relaxed after all their dancing.

"But maybe they have the right idea, Andy," Matt said in his shy way. "Maybe parties are meant for a kiss or two."

Andy's eyebrows went up. "Well, maybe you're right," she agreed. She snuggled closer to Matt, touching the collar of his silly beach shirt, and their mouths came together in a kiss.

"So that's what parties are for," Andy said. Sometimes a serious boy like Matt could be quite talented at a serious thing like kissing.

"Looks like nobody's feeling like a wall-flower over here," commented Toby, pushing through the peanuts sand with Neal to join her roommates.

"I'd say our party is a major success," Andy declared, beaming with joy at the whole group.

"The only sad thing," Jane said, "is that Gigi couldn't be here with us."

"I know," Toby said, shaking her head. "It just isn't the same without her."

The next night, all the girls of Baker House threw one more party — in honor of Gigi Norton.

The meal in the dining hall was to be informal that evening, with a buffet of sand-wiches and salads. Canby Hall Sunday suppers were served that way when Ms. Merriweather had her weekend off to go and visit her grandchildren. People wondered whether Ms. Merriweather did the cooking when she went visiting her relatives, but that was simply too scary to think about. Whatever happened on Ms. Merriweather visits, the dining hall in her absence was a very popular place, packed with hungry students.

Gigi and Yolanda arrived at the dining hall just as the doors opened, but they were surprised to see that no one from Baker House was there.

"Well, this should be a treat," Gigi said to Yolanda and several other girls from Addison. "With luck, we'll be spared the company of those peasants from Baker!"

No sooner had she spoken, than the double doors of the dining room swung open with a flourish. In walked the entire population of Baker House.

"What's going on?" asked Heide Fraser, staring.

Every single Baker girl was wearing a black wig. More precisely, every girl was wearing the stringy part of a five-and-dime mop, and each mop had been dyed jet black, the same midnight black color as Gigi Norton's hair.

"And look at all the makeup they're wearing," Yolanda commented, squinting her eyes. "Sort of like what you wear, Gigi."

"Shut up, Yo," Gigi hissed.

The dozens of black-haired, overly made-up Baker House girls went marching around the dining hall, humming softly a song that sounded like, "If You Knew Gigi like We Know Gigi. . . ."

At the end of the parade, the three girls from 407 marched in carrying a huge sign on a mop handle. Gigi read the sign and her jaw dropped. She looked frantically around, but no one, not even Yolanda, seemed ready to sympathize with her outrage. Red-faced, she turned and went marching out of the dining hall, her back straight and stiff.

The sign said:

"COSTUME PARADE! COME DRESSED AS SOMEONE YOU'D LIKE TO SHIP OFF TO A DESERT ISLAND — WITH A ONE-WAY TICKET!"

"Well, I guess we did all right with Plan E," Jane said later that evening in Room 409. Six of them were gathered there to help Dee repair her palm tree, which they were embellishing with all sorts of jungle foliage. Pretty soon the entire room would resemble a South American rain forest, but Dee and Maggie didn't seem to mind in the least.

Laura Lee chuckled at the memory of "The Getting Even with Gigi Plan."

"Well, she deserved all that," Andy said, "and more. She's just lucky I didn't go to Ms. Allardyce with that story."

"Yes, she sure is," Jane said, putting the finishing touches on a big tropical plant she'd painted over the window. "And by the way, has anybody heard the weather forecast at all?"

"I have," Toby said in a gloomy voice. "We're going to have at least six more weeks of winter, they're saying."

Five heads swiveled to look at Toby.

Toby put on a good act. She stared at her feet, shuffled them a little bit, and tried to look sad. But suddenly she was grinning widely. "Just kidding! Spring is here, and I have all you terrific people as friends!"

"Hear, hear," Laura Lee said, raising a can of soda toward Toby and the others. "I totally agree. You guys are what make Canby Hall really fantastic. You are the best bunch of friends that anyone could ever hope for."

Jane smiled, a warm, secret, personal sort of smile. She felt pretty good, actually. They had helped Toby to conquer her Winter Blahs and they had helped to make Laura Lee see that it was more fun to be with people than to be a hermit.

Which just went to prove, Jane thought, what a powerful force friendship could be.

The staff of Canby Hall goes on strike. Can the girls of 407 keep the school from closing down, and the big carnival from being called off? To find out, read The Girls of Canby Hall Super Edition, THE ALMOST SUMMER CARNIVAL.

Read All About The Girls of Canby Hall!

Get ready for friends...
Get ready for fun...
Get ready for...

JUNIOR HIGH

Get ready for a fresh new year of 8th grade madness at Cedar Groves Junior High! Laugh at best friends Nora and Jen's "cool" attempts to fit in. Cringe at the exceptionally gross tricks of Jason, the class nerd. Be awed by Mia who shows up on the first day dressed in a punk outfit. And meet Denise, "Miss Sophistication," who shocks Nora and Jen by suggesting they invite *BOYS* to the Halloween party!

Get ready for **JUNIOR HIGH**, a new series about the funny side of life in junior high school.

Look for these new Junior High titles at your nearest bookstore!
$2.25 U.S./$2.95 CAN.

JUNIOR HIGH JITTERS #1 by M.L. Kennedy

CLASS CRUSH #2 by Kate Kenyon

THE DAY THE EIGHTH GRADE RAN THE SCHOOL #3 by Kate Kenyon

HOW DUMB CAN YOU GET? #4 by Kate Kenyon

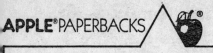